Sweet America

An Immigrant's Story

-"I love sweet America. They are kind to me here."
—Rosie, P.S. 188

Steven Kroll

JAMESTOWN PUBLISHERS

a division of NTC/CONTEMPORARY PUBLISHING GROUP
Lincolnwood, Illinois USA

For my wife, sweet Kathleen

Two important thank yous. To Mary Elizabeth Brown
of the Center for Migration Studies, Staten Island, New York
whose knowledge and guidance helped get this book started.
And to my editor, Juliette Underwood Looye, who solves
every problem and gets everything right.

Cover Credits
  Design: Herman Adler Design Group
  Illustration: David Schweitzer
  Timeline: (left) Robert Amft; (middle) North Wind;
  (right) Gamma Liaison

  Page 172: © Museum of the City of New York

ISBN: 0-8092-0580-7 (hardbound)
ISBN: 0-8092-0622-6 (softbound)

Published by JamestownPublishers,
a division of NTC/Contemporary Publishing Group, Inc.,
4255 West Touhy Avenue,
Lincolnwood (Chicago), Illinois 60646-1975 U.S.A.
© 2000 by Steven Kroll

90 ML 0 9 8 7 6 5 4 3 2 1

Manhattan's Lower East Side 1899

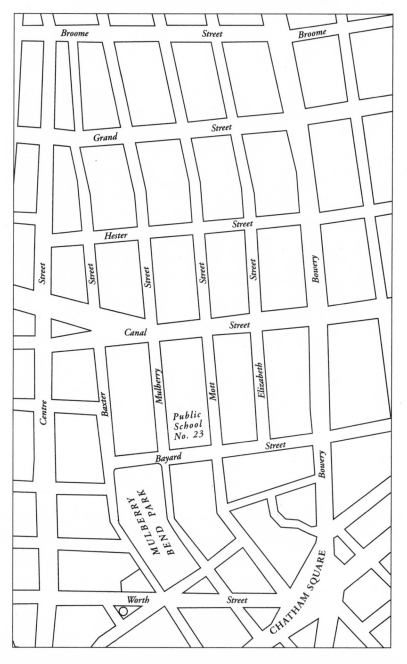

Prologue

"No!"

Tony shouted at his father and ran out of the apartment. He slammed the door and pounded five flights down to the street.

It was like going down a chute. The stairs were narrow, dark, and steep. They also smelled very bad—of cooking food and toilets on each landing that were never very clean.

Tony held his breath and gripped the banister. His feet flew over the creaky stairs, just missing the broken one halfway down. He burst through the downstairs door, but he didn't go far. He sat down hard on the tenement's front steps.

It was after dark on Mulberry Street, but there were people everywhere. The pushcarts and organ grinders were gone, but older boys still lingered on the corner, and the cafes and restaurants, along with the saloons, were busy. People were going in and out, laughing and shouting, banging doors. Some of the cafes were open to the street. Their tables, filled mostly with Italians, spilled out onto the pavement. A lot of older people had dragged chairs outside. They sat, talking in little groups. On a hot June night, no one wanted to be in a tenement apartment.

Tony looked out at the people enjoying one another's company, and he couldn't believe what he had done. He had refused to obey his father's wish. He had talked back to him, been rude and insolent. He never should have disobeyed his papà! That was something a son did not do.

In his mind, he saw his father's angry face—the face he'd seen as he ran out the door. Big and broad, Pietro was sitting at the kitchen table in his undershirt. His eyes blazed, and he turned away from his son.

Tony felt as if he'd been thrown out of his family. His family: the most important thing in the world to him. He was nothing without his mamma and papà, his two brothers, and his sister. They were the only people he could count on, the only ones he knew he could trust.

But how could he agree to work full-time, to be a *full-time* newsboy?

He'd been in America for more than two years. He'd gone to school and learned English and graduated from eighth grade. He wanted to keep going to school to learn a trade or a profession. He'd agreed to work part-time as a newsboy to help earn money for the family, but he wanted to go farther, be more successful, do something interesting.

Papà said no. Papà said, in Italian, "Enough! You must give more to the family."

And that was when Tony said no.

Chapter 1

He was medium height and slim, with warm dark eyes and a sharp nose. His name was Antonio Petrosino, but everyone in America called him Tony. Everyone except his family, who still called him Tonio.

When he arrived in New York City in the spring of 1887, he was twelve years old. His brothers, Vincenzo and Giuseppe, were ten and eight. His little sister Angelina was just six. They came from Teggiano, a little village outside Naples in the province of Salerno. They came with their mamma when the letter arrived from the *padrone*.

The *padrone*—sometimes dishonest and sometimes not—provided services for Italian immigrants. Papà had gone to New York two years earlier, and the letter said he had found a good job and an apartment. It enclosed steamship tickets on the White Star Line.

Tonio was excited.

"Mamma," he shouted, "we have a poster from the White Star Line on our wall!"

Mamma nodded. The poster showed a beautiful white ship steaming off into the sun. Tonio had looked at it—stared at it—so many times. He'd looked at it whenever he thought of escape.

Life in Teggiano was hard. The family lived in a one-room cottage with peeling walls and a stone floor. There were a couple of chairs and a small portable stove to cook on. The only light came from opening the door, and most of the space was taken up by a large iron bed. Everyone slept in the bed. When Angelina was a baby, she had dangled from the ceiling in a reed basket suspended by ropes.

Mamma had hung a crucifix beside the poster. There was an outhouse in the yard behind the house. Every day before dawn, the family got up to work the land that belonged to the rich man who lived on the hill. Tonio milked the cow. Sometimes, when the winds were fierce, the farm animals slept in the house to help keep everyone warm.

There were droughts too, and taxes they couldn't pay, and everything got worse after Papà left. The family missed him terribly, and it was harder to get things done. But the truth was, this peasant life—the life of the *contadini*—couldn't get much worse.

So Tonio was excited when the letter came, but he was also very scared. He'd never known anything but

Teggiano, he didn't speak English, and America was a very big and scary place.

They got their passports without any trouble. It seemed easier because Papà was already in America. They got new clothes—a colorful shirt for Tonio and a shawl for Mamma. Tonio had never had such clothes before. Then Uncle Giorgio gave them a special dinner and suddenly, in a rush, they were on the train to Naples.

Looking out the window, clutching little Angelina's hand, Tonio wondered if he would ever see this dark earth, this dark sky again. Many Italian men did return from their journeys to America—some with money, more without. But Tonio was going to grow up there, not just take a job. His story, he felt, was going to be different.

In Naples, they were herded into a crumbling old hotel near the waterfront, jammed together into a small room with two other families. One of the babies cried constantly, so nobody got much sleep. Tonio wouldn't have slept anyway. His excitement and his fear were raging in him now.

Years later, he would realize that this was the moment when privacy vanished from his childhood. In Teggiano, if the little cottage seemed too crowded or if he just wanted to be by himself, all he had to do was walk out into the fields and take a deep breath. From now on, there would be no empty, open space. Wherever he went, there would be crowds.

The next morning, the waterfront was so packed with people it took several hours to reach the ship. Pickpockets worked the crowd, but Tonio protected Mamma's knitted bag and helped keep the younger children close.

Papà's letter from the *padrone* had warned Mamma against thieves, but a man appeared selling grass ropes to secure the immigrants' flimsy cloth and paper luggage. He looked honest. The ropes were cheap. Mamma bought one and tied it around their suitcase.

A moment later, Vincenzo was yelling, "Mamma, mamma, over there!"

An old woman was loaded down with caps. They were red and green and gold.

Mamma shook her head. "Not now, Vincenzo. We will buy your next cap in America."

She did not even know if there would be enough money for bread.

Pushed and prodded from all sides, trying to hold on to Giuseppe and Angelina, Tonio looked up at the ship. It didn't look as grand as the one in the poster. It seemed smaller and older. But now, as they got closer, other men appeared, trying to sell baggage labels or vaccination certificates or change *lire* into dollars at a scandalous profit.

Mamma pulled the children away. When they reached the ship and had their papers checked, they were immediately sent below decks to steerage, as low as you could get above the waterline.

Climbing down the stairs, Tonio felt like he was descending into a nightmare. The space was cramped and would have been completely dark had it not been for the occasional smudged porthole. The smell was musty and fetid, though not as bad as it would get after weeks without baths or toilets. Closely spaced rows of three-tiered iron beds were divided into groups. The mattresses were burlap-covered straw, and some were full of bugs. People were rushing to the beds so fast that it was all Mamma and Tonio could do to keep the family together.

The voyage took two-and-a half weeks. There were storms and people got seasick, huddled like animals in their filthy bunks. The food—salted meat, potatoes, rotten fish—was so bad that Tonio could hardly eat. Only when he could find a place for Mamma and the others up on deck—when the wind whipped through their clothes and the stars shone overhead—did it become possible for him to forget what he was eating and swallow it.

Angelina got sick and cried for days. Giuseppe got into a fight and had his nose bloodied. Tonio just tried to hang on.

Mostly he stayed with his family, but at the end of the second week he made a friend. To avoid the stench below, he had sneaked up on deck during the day.

A crew member taunted him. "Hey, wop! Hey, dago!"

Tonio had never heard those words before, though he would certainly hear them again. He was holding on tight to the rail, looking out over the ocean and trying not to listen when he noticed another boy beside him.

"How do you stand it?" the boy asked in Italian. "Is this what it will be like in America?"

Tonio shrugged. He had no answers, but the next

moment they were talking. The boy's name was Tomasso Battaglia. He was from a village not far from Teggiano. His father was also in New York City, but Tomasso was an only child. He was making the trip with his mother, but she was not feeling well.

Tonio and Tomasso became inseparable. They wandered around the ship and played tricks on the wretched crew. Mamma got a little testy over Tonio's long absences, but by then the voyage was nearly over and Tonio lost track of Tomasso in the crowded confusion of arrival.

The ship steamed into New York Harbor. Squeezing up on deck, apologizing as he clambered over others less intent, Tonio got to the rail to see the recently installed Statue of Liberty. The arm holding the torch, the beautifully set crown—never had he seen anything so beautiful. He raced down the stairs to tell the others.

They reached a Manhattan pier. Doctors came on board to inspect their vaccination certificates and to examine their eyes for a contagious disease called trachoma. A few passengers were not allowed to leave the ship, but the rest were taken to a large round building on the Battery called Castle Garden.

Castle Garden had been a fort during the War of 1812 and then a concert hall. Now it was big and dark and dusty. Tonio looked up and noticed streaks of light slanting through the ceiling.

The room was already full of people from earlier ships. They sat on benches and railings and on the floor. Over on the side were booths selling railroad tickets and tables with food to buy. Tonio wanted to look, but Mamma wouldn't let go of his hand.

Up ahead, inspectors sat on tall stools. Standing in line with his family, inching closer to the stools, Tonio's fears increased. They'd come so far and left their homes behind. They'd suffered so much. What if they were sent back? What if Papà wasn't there to meet them and they were alone in America?

They seemed to have been standing there forever. Vincenzo was getting hungry. Angelina began to whine. Finally they reached an inspector.

He was very thin. He was wearing a uniform. He had pale hair and blue eyes that stared at them coldly through rimless glasses. Beside him stood a chubby little man who turned out to be an interpreter.

Tonio had never seen a man who looked like the inspector before. Mamma smiled. The inspector did not.

He examined their passports. He began firing questions: How old are you? How old are your children? Are you married? Where will you live? How much money do you have? Who is waiting for you?

With this last question, Mamma squared her shoulders. "My husband," she said, beaming.

The inspector hardly paid attention. "All right," he said, "let them through." And they were released into Battery Park, New York City, America.

Chapter 2

And there was Papà.

"Pietro!" Mamma shouted and rushed into his arms.

Tonio and the others gathered around, jostling one another for position, each wanting to be closest to their father. And when Papà stopped embracing Mamma, he hugged and kissed each one of the children, asking how they were and how the journey had gone. But with Angelina, he hoisted her into the air, laughing and shouting, "My little one, my little one, you are so pretty!"

Angelina shrieked with joy. It was the first time in weeks that she'd seemed happy.

With Tonio, Papà asked, "So, did you look after your mamma?"

Tonio had never thought to do anything else. "*Si*, Papà, of course."

And then it was time to go home—to their new home

in America, the apartment Papà had found for them on Mulberry Street. He would take them there. Carrying the battered suitcase, he led them out of Battery Park and away from the hordes of new arrivals; the thieves; and the runners offering cheap hotel rooms, boarding houses, hot meals, money changing.

They started up through the tumult of Broadway: the crowds, the shops, the horse cars pulled along rails down the middle of the street, the garbage and manure piled on the cobblestones. Tonio marveled at the tall buildings several stories high. He stared at the men in their top hats and derbies and the women in their long dresses pinched at the waist. All the while, his father was talking, explaining, filling his family in on two nearly missing years.

Papà had sent so few letters because he had not wanted to alarm anyone. Also, he had so little money he could not afford to pay the *padrone* to have letters written. He had left with so much hope, they knew, but they also knew that he had been robbed on the waterfront in Naples and had arrived in New York City after that terrible journey with almost nothing.

Luigi Mazzaferri, their cousin from Teggiano, had met Papà at Castle Garden. It was a good thing he did. Otherwise, those thieves and cheats who hung around the Battery and hustled every unprotected immigrant would have taken the little Papà had left. Luigi took him straight to a boarding house on Mulberry Street, the same street they would be living on now. The boarding house was run by a woman who was also from Teggiano. For a few cents, she gave Papà a clean bed and a good meal.

The next day Luigi brought Papà to the *padrone*, whose office was in the front of a saloon. The *padrone* was fat and bald and a little too enthusiastic. When Papà tried to clarify details, the *padrone* leaned back in his chair and said, "You want a job, you listen to me."

Papà listened and, for a fee, took the train with a hundred other men to a quarry in Vermont. There, with a strong arm, he broke stones day after day. He earned even less than he had expected because each week the company told him he'd worked fewer hours than he knew he had.

He lived crammed into a boxcar with 10 other workers. It got cold at night, and the bedding was full of lice and beetles. What scraps the men could find to eat, they cooked over an open fire.

After three months, Papà was back in New York. The *padrone* found him work unloading barges on the Hudson River docks. Once again, he stayed in the Mulberry Street boarding house. The work was tough and dirty, and he missed his family. But finally, after a year, he had a better job, laying streets near Central Park. He was making $1.50 a day. With the rest of the family working when they could, they would be all right.

By now, with Mamma nodding and the children listening, they had reached Grand Street. Absorbed in his father's story, Tonio couldn't help noticing the store windows full of furniture and linens and fancy clothes— just like the clothes people had been wearing on Broadway.

And then they were on Mulberry Street, walking north toward Broome. Tonio would never forget his first view of the block he would call home. It came at him with such force that he was overwhelmed.

There were shops with awnings and shops without, shops with fruit and vegetables or clothes or shoes overflowing onto the street. There were fire escapes with laundry hanging across them. There were horses and wagons, delivery boys, flower sellers, and organ grinders with their monkeys. There were women with baskets on their heads and women shouting from windows. There were cafes and restaurants. There were peddlers with pushcarts and movable stands, selling fish, candy, shirts, and suspenders. Down the middle of the street, where space permitted, people were slowly moving. And everywhere there were children—children playing marbles or shooting dice in an alley or gathered together on the corner or running and running.

Papà took Mamma's hand. She was uncertain, fearful. She held on tight to Angelina with her other hand. Tonio, swallowing hard, made sure that Vincenzo and Giuseppe did not wander off or get swept away. In the last weeks they had all become accustomed to crowds, but never before had they encountered so much pulsing diversity in one place.

"Many of the people living on this block come from our Salerno province or from Teggiano," Papà said proudly.

Mamma smiled, trying to avoid getting bumped on

one side or trampled on the other. Taking it all in, Tonio was suddenly knocked to the ground by a fleeing child, barefoot and wearing short pants. Papà rushed to help, but Tonio wasn't hurt, merely shaken. He got to his feet and brushed himself off.

And then, halfway down the block, they were there. A trip that had taken only minutes seemed to have lasted hours. Climbing between two pushcarts with huge wheels, Papà led his family to their building. He went to open the door, but it opened for him. Standing in the doorway was a tall boy about Tonio's age.

Papà looked blank. He had met most of his neighbors, but he obviously hadn't met this one.

"Salvatore Amalfi, from Padula," the boy said, extending his hand.

Immediately, Papà broke into a grin. Padula wasn't far from Teggiano. There were stories to share and probably people in common. He took the boy's hand and wished him a good day. "*Buon giorno*," he said, "*buon giorno*." Then he introduced Mamma and the children.

When Papà introduced Tonio, Salvatore said in Italian, "I hope to get to know you better. I will come back later, when you are more settled."

Silently, Tonio rejoiced. He had only just arrived in this wonderful, strange country, and already he was making a friend. "*Grazie*," he said and smiled. Then he followed Papà, Mamma, his brothers and his sister into the dark hallway of the building that would be their new home.

It was a "dumbbell" style tenement—six stories high with four apartments on a floor. It was called a dumbbell because a narrow central airshaft and a narrow, dark stairway made it thinner in the middle than at the ends. As Tonio climbed that stairway for the first time, it seemed forbidding and creepy with its creaking wooden stairs, its smelly toilets, its puckered walls in the murky darkness. And there was the endlessness of the climb, floor after floor into forever, climbing single file. But then they reached the fifth floor. The door to their apartment was thrown open, and they were inside.

"Ten dollars a month," Papà announced.

It was a rear apartment with three small square rooms set one behind the other. There were two windows at the far end. Vincenzo and Giuseppe rushed to look out but saw only the wall of another tenement. The other rooms, with tiny windows on the airshaft, had almost no light. But there were beds in the back two rooms, and the front room—the one off the hall—had a stove and a sink!

Mamma was pleased. Tonio was pleased. This was not a terrific home, he realized, but it was better than Teggiano. They had more than one room and more than one bed. They had windows and water and toilets inside the house. In Teggiano, they had none of these things.

"We want to sleep in the back room!" Vincenzo and Giuseppe shouted.

It was decided that the three boys would sleep in the back room. Mamma, Papà, and Angelina would sleep in the middle room. The front room—the one with the stove and the sink—would be the kitchen and family

15

room. It would be the room where people would sit and visit.

Mamma and the children unpacked the suitcase. Mamma hung the crucifix on her bedroom wall. They began to feel at home. Papà went out and bought pasta and sausage for supper.

Later, Salvatore came by for Tonio. No, he wouldn't keep him out late. He realized it was their first night in America.

He took Tonio to a "Cheap Charlie." It was a candy store on the corner called the Napoli, where the neighborhood boys liked to meet, horse around, play cards, even perform. No one was performing that night, but Salvatore bought Tonio a soda from the fountain and some gumdrops from the row of glass containers on the counter. He explained that he had been in America a little less than a year, that he was learning English and working part-time as a newsboy.

"Being a newsboy is a good thing," he said. "But first you must learn English. Then you can do anything."

Tonio wasn't so sure about selling newspapers on the street, but he knew that Salvatore was right about English. He would get to that as soon as he could—as soon as he could start school and learn to read and write.

It was nice to have a friend in America, Tonio thought, someone who liked him enough to want to offer advice so soon after they'd met. He wondered what was happening to Tomasso, the boy he had met aboard ship.

As Tonio and Salvatore were talking, a group of tough-looking boys stormed into the candy store. They took over a few tables and sprawled in their chairs. A couple of them came over to talk with Salvatore. They called him Sal and spoke only in English. Tonio couldn't understand them, but when they got to "Who's the new guy?" and pointed at him, the meaning was clear.

Sal explained who Tonio was.

"Will he want to join us?" asked one of them, tough and obviously a leader.

"How can I know?" Sal said. "Give him a little time, Paul."

Paul shrugged and walked away.

A boy with a mustache and a peaked cap said, "Hey, let's go to Nunzio's. I want something to drink."

When the group had gone, Salvatore told Tonio about the gangs in New York City. He described how the Italian gangs protected other Italians—mostly from the Irish. And he explained that Tonio would have to decide if he wanted to belong or not.

This gang was called the Wayfarers. They tried to guard their turf and had Americanized their names. He'd be Tony soon enough in America, but he'd be Tony right away if he joined the gang.

But some of the gangs were also a bad thing. They terrorized neighborhoods, and sometimes they stole from people or beat them up. The Wayfarers weren't so bad. They were more like a social club. But they could get nasty, and some of the boys didn't go to school or hold down regular jobs. They might make Tonio steal a piece of fruit from a pushcart before he could join.

Was Salvatore a member?

"No, I don't like gangs. But I stay friendly, even when they needle me. It's the only way to get by."

Later that night, in bed beside his two brothers, Tonio went over in his mind the events of this unbelievable day. From landing at Castle Garden to joining Papà after so long, from seeing Broadway and Mulberry Street and the apartment to meeting Salvatore and the Wayfarers. It was all so dazzling and strange, uncertain and new. How would he fit in? How would it work out? There was only one thing he knew for sure: he wasn't ready to be Tony.

Chapter 3

The next morning: reality. Papà had to get up at five-thirty to go to work. The fare on the horse cars was five cents. Papà couldn't afford it, so he had to walk blocks and blocks uptown. Then, after a whole day with pick and shovel, he had to walk home.

Most Italians tried to live as close to their work as they could, but Papà had waited for this job and he wanted to keep it. He seldom got home before dark. He was tired and often angry, but he never once talked about quitting.

Already that first morning, the tiny apartment seemed darker and more cramped. There was no room for the younger children, no room for Mamma or Papà or Tonio. In Teggiano it had been worse, of course, but in Teggiano you could just walk outside. Here on Mulberry Street, they were five flights from the ground. How could they possibly keep going up and down?

Within a few short weeks, Mamma got over these feelings. She began to make a life for her family in America that she never would have dreamed possible. Back in Italy, she never left her village. She stayed with her family and almost never saw anyone else. Now things had to be different.

First she had to meet the neighbors. This was less scary than it could have been, since everyone in the building came from a village near Teggiano and spoke Italian.

Mamma knew she would meet them all eventually, but the hallway was so dark and the stairway so narrow, it might take months. She took the children. She walked across the hall. A thin woman beaming with sunny charm, she knocked on the door of the front apartment. The name on the door said Biondo.

The door opened. Mamma held out her hand, the way Americans did. Signora Teresa Petrosino introduced herself to Signora Giuseppina Biondo. Then she introduced the children. Tonio was embarrassed and hardly said a word. They were all invited inside for espresso and talk of the Old Country and the neighborhood.

Giuseppina explained that her husband was a barber and that they had five children. Whenever Teresa wanted to look for her children in the street, she could look out Giuseppina's window.

Mamma made these introductions several times. On the fourth floor she met Mrs. Mirabelli, whose husband was a bootblack; on the third floor, Mrs. Pacci, whose husband was a fruit peddler; and on the second floor, Mrs. Amalfi, who was Salvatore's mother and whose husband was a laborer.

Salvatore was at home with his two sisters when the Petrosinos arrived, but he, like Tonio, didn't say much. Instead, they looked at the wall in embarrassment as their mothers talked. Signora Amalfi adored Signora Petrosino, just as everyone else had.

In this way, Mamma not only made new friends. She also found out where to shop for everything the family needed—from fish and sausage to pasta, fruit, and vegetables. Then she went and introduced herself to the shopkeepers. She also learned where to get work she and the children could do at home.

It was August and still the slow season for garment-making. Mamma took the children and went over to the Alpha Flower Company on East Houston Street. A manager there spoke Italian. It didn't take much for Mamma to convince him to give her and the children work.

The manager piled up the boxes of artificial flower parts. The younger children carried one apiece, while Mamma and Tonio each carried three. Cradling the boxes in their arms, it was almost impossible for them to negotiate the crowds of Mulberry Street. Somehow they made it home. Starting up the stairs, Angelina grimaced. "I can't do it."

"Don't worry, little one," Tonio whispered, "I will

come back for yours."

A small secondhand sofa and a table and chairs were in the front room now. All had been bought on credit. Mamma had pinned a calendar and pictures of the saints above the sofa and placed doilies on the shelves of the cabinets. Laundry soap and Bon Ami cleanser sat on the edge of the sink. Mamma had heard that Italians were supposed to be dirty, but she was having none of it. The apartment was cramped but spotless. They had no bathtub, but everyone got a sponge bath twice a week.

The boxes of artificial flowers thumped onto the table. Everyone set to work, fitting roses on stems, pasting petals, adding centers to daisies. The pay was eight cents a gross, which was twelve dozen flowers. A little more was paid if there were extra petals. Working hard, the family could earn six or seven dollars a week.

With not enough room for everyone at the table, Tonio and Vincenzo worked on the floor.

After an hour, Vincenzo groaned. "Oh, Mamma" he said, his fingers covered in paste, "this is terrible."

"Yes," said Mamma, "I know, but it is the best we can do right now."

She did better for them even then. Keeping Angelina with her because the child was so little, Mamma sent the boys outside to play every afternoon. And play they did—whooping as they flew down the stairs, racing outside to explore the few blocks of their neighborhood.

Tonio looked after his brothers, but there was almost nothing they couldn't do together. They learned to play marbles and dice. They played leapfrog in the middle of the street and baseball one block over on Mott, using manhole covers and ash barrels and sometimes even an old man named Johnny as the bases.

They met Carlo and Stefano and Federico, who called themselves Carl and Steve and Freddy. Once, Carlo said he didn't think Giuseppe should play baseball because he was too young. Tonio said, "If he doesn't play, I don't play." Tonio was a good player, and that was that—Giuseppe played.

When Mamma gave the boys money, they went to the Napoli candy store on the corner. Tonio was developing a taste for Jujyfruits.

And the three of them followed policemen down the street, the way the other kids did. They wandered in and out of shops and around the pushcarts, looking at things they couldn't buy. From time to time, Tonio noticed the Wayfarers gathered on the corner, but he made sure they didn't notice him noticing.

Sometimes Salvatore joined Tonio and his brothers, and those times were always the best.

In the evenings after dinner, the family went back to work, assembling the flowers by gaslight until nine or ten at night. Sometimes Papà tried to help, but his fingers were thick and clumsy and he had trouble holding the petals.

At other times, Papà was so tired he fell asleep on the sofa. But the moments Tonio liked best were when Papà talked about his job: digging up the ground, shoveling in the gravel, laying the square paving stones on top.

Every so often, Luigi Mazzaferri stopped by for a visit. He was the cousin who had met Papà at Castle Garden on his first day in America. Tonio didn't like Luigi. He thought Luigi tried too hard and would say or do anything for attention. But Luigi was their relative and Papà's friend, so he was always welcome.

Sometimes Luigi insisted upon giving a performance. He would stand up in the middle of the little front room and recite a famous poem. Or he would pretend to be Garibaldi, the great soldier who had unified Italy in 1861. He would dance around, gesturing and shouting.

Papà would always laugh. Mamma would shake her head. At those moments, Tonio knew he was right about Luigi.

Then it was time to start school. Tonio would always remember that first day. Mamma had them all up early. They were scrubbed and dressed. They had eaten breakfast.

But Mamma wouldn't take them. Instead she looked at the floor.

"You take them, Tonio," she said in halting Italian. "You are the oldest."

"But Mamma—"

"Go ahead now. You don't want to be late the first day."

Tonio understood that Mamma was embarrassed to go to the school. He didn't want her to be—he was very proud of her—but he also realized that nothing he could do was going to change her mind. "Yes, Mamma," he said, and he led the children down the stairs.

Although it was early, Mulberry Street was already jammed with people. Someone was selling apples from a wagon. A flower seller was setting up. A bootblack was busy on the corner. The pushcart peddlers were lined up along the curbs.

Mrs. Mirabelli was already bargaining for potatoes right outside their front door. "*Buon giorno, bambini*," she said as Tonio, Vincenzo, Giuseppe, and Angelina passed by.

"*Buon giorno*, Signora Mirabelli," they all replied.

Tonio held tightly to Angelina's hand as they made their way down Mulberry Street, past Hester and Canal, to the corner of Bayard Street and Public School number 23. It was a gray day, nothing terribly inviting, and Tonio remembered how he'd felt as they dodged among the peddlers and the pedestrians. He wanted so much to learn everything he could, but he had never been to school. He was so afraid of going that he wasn't sure he'd even get there.

Also, P.S. 23 was right at the edge of the notorious Mulberry Bend, known to everyone as New York City's worst slum. A labyrinth of dying buildings, basement saloons, filthy streets, and wicked people, it sprawled south of Bayard Street and around the elbow in Mulberry that gave it its name. Even as he'd begun wandering a block or two from his home, Tonio had been warned to stay away from the Bend. But now here he was, leading his brothers and sister right to the edge of it. And that was where they would go to school!

They reached the building. It was big and imposing, with a gray stone front. Lots of other children were arriving. Hurriedly they climbed the stairs, ignoring as best they could the beaten-down tenements across the street.

"Are you ready?" Tonio asked the others as they reached the top step.

They nodded. He'd never seen them look so pale, not even on the ship to America.

He opened the door—to pandemonium! There were so many children, parents, and teachers crowded into the entrance and corridors of the school that it was almost impossible to breathe. Somehow in this sea of people, Tonio was able to find someone who spoke Italian and could tell him what rooms the four of them were in. He was reminded of the Atlantic crossing all over again.

He told Vincenzo and Giuseppe where they should go and watched them disappear into the crowded corridor, holding each other's hands. He led Angelina to her first-grade classroom and got her seated. Then he went to his own.

It was a third-grade class.

Angelina was six. Tonio was twelve. She was in first grade, he was in third. Of course he was humiliated, but he also understood. He had to start somewhere. Why didn't they just put him in first grade as well?

He entered the classroom. It was a dim, cavernous space with dirty windows, grimy green walls, and a dark wooden floor. There were rows of wooden desks with wooden chairs behind them. The desk and chairs had iron legs. They were all nailed to the floor.

Tonio sat down in one of the chairs. His knees bumped up against the small desk. Moments later, another boy was there, squeezing in and sharing his seat.

The room kept filling up with children. Soon everyone was sharing a desk, a chair, a seat on the floor. As Tonio sat sandwiched between more and more eight- and nine-year-olds, he noticed a number of others his age. He also became aware of an awful smell—a combination of sweaty bodies, neglected bathrooms, and decaying building.

The teacher's name was Miss McGowen. The first day of school was a half-day. There were so many children and so much confusion as to who belonged where, it took most of that time just to call the roll. Also, there were angry parents in the hall, complaining that even though they lived in the neighborhood, P.S. 23 was too full to admit their children. The shouting didn't help keep things under control.

Finally Miss McGowen, who had bright red hair and seemed very young, reached the last names beginning with P. Tonio got ready. He listened very hard for his name.

"Tony Petrosino," Miss McGowen said.

Tonio couldn't believe it. He was Tony now—Tony

already. It didn't have anything to do with the Wayfarers. It had happened by itself. He was Tony in his own right, here at school and anywhere else he would go.

"Tony Petrosino," Miss McGowen repeated.

"Si!" Tony shouted, then "Yes!" only a little more softly.

He was Tony—Tony learning English, Tony the American.

Chapter 4

When Tonio—now Tony—got out of school, he waited for his brothers and sister on the corner of Bayard Street. He realized that it was probably a mistake to be standing at this dangerous edge of Mulberry Bend, but what could he do? Throngs of children were pouring through the front doors of P.S. 23. There was nowhere else to wait.

Vincenzo, Giuseppe, and Angelina seemed to be taking a long time. Tony shifted from one foot to the other, watching disheveled men and women wandering in and out of the alleyways of the Bend. He was dimly aware of a group of older boys milling around across the street.

Suddenly they were in front of him. They weren't just a group, they were a gang. And from their hulking manner and notorious black clothes, they weren't just any gang. They were the Ragpickers from Baxter Street.

They were Irish. Their leader was a tough named Harry Hickey, who had done time in jail.

Tony looked up into the face of a barrel-chested boy with cold blue eyes, a pug nose, and a square jaw. He was wearing a black bowler hat and black suspenders.

It had to be Hickey.

The boy said, "Hey, wop!" and pushed Tony hard.

Tony's mouth dropped open. Shocked, not speaking English, he didn't know what to do.

"What're you doin' on our corner?" the boy continued, pushing him again.

This time, Tony fell. He wanted to fight back, to show how angry he was at this injustice, but he was helpless.

The boy stood over him, large and powerful. "Listen to me, wop! I'm Hickey, I'm the leader. Don't you ever do nothin' that gets in our way, you hear? The Ragpickers'll run you out of town if you do."

As suddenly as they had appeared, they were gone. Tony picked himself up. He wondered why they had attacked him and what they could possibly have against him, beyond the fact that he was Italian and standing on the wrong corner. That, he suspected, was enough, no matter how foolish it seemed.

They knew him now. He'd have to be careful. The thought of joining the Wayfarers for safety briefly crossed his mind, but he wouldn't do it. They weren't for him. He didn't like the violence or the attitude.

He brushed off his clothes. His brothers and sister were approaching. He didn't want them to know what had happened. He wouldn't say anything at home either.

Winding their way through the crowds on the way back to Mulberry Street, Vincenzo and Giuseppe chattered about being in the same class even though they were different ages, and about how their classmates were all younger than they were. Since Tony had it even worse, he wasn't too sympathetic.

"Learn," he said finally in Italian. "The rest will take care of itself."

Entering their building, they met Salvatore.

"Where were you?" Tony asked. "I looked for you at school."

Salvatore explained that he had gone in early. He was in seventh grade this year and wanted to be sure he wouldn't be turned away.

"Can we meet later?" Tony asked.

"Sure," said Salvatore, "later."

At the top of the narrow stairs, Mamma was waiting. As each of her children appeared, she hugged and kissed them. "Students," she said in Italian, "you are all students."

Then she served a lunch of eggs and potatoes. While they ate, Tony announced that he was no longer Tonio. He was now Tony because of his teacher.

"She called me Tony in front of the whole class!" he shouted.

Vincenzo and Giuseppe were surprised. Mamma said it was fine, just fine. She would probably forget and call him Tonio, but it was all right to want to be an American already as long as he didn't forget he was Italian.

Thinking of the Ragpickers, Tony said, "No, Mamma, never. I will not forget."

To celebrate this special day, Mamma sent the boys outside for the afternoon. No flower making today. No paste on the fingers and under the nails. The only catch was they had to take Angelina.

Mamma returned to her work as the four of them tore down the stairs, Tony holding back a little because Angelina was riding on his shoulders. They picked up Salvatore on the way and raced out the door.

Over on Mott Street, Carl and Steve—Tony could call them that now—were ready to play ball. Tony parked Angelina on the curb to watch and then immediately snagged a ball that might have gone for a triple at least.

Later, waiting to come to bat, Tony confided in Salvatore. When he mentioned his name change from Tonio to Tony, his friend's face brightened. He punched Tony on the arm. "Now you can call me Sal."

But when Tony mentioned the Ragpickers, there was silence. Finally Sal said, "You don't want to mess with Harry Hickey."

"I won't," said Tony. "I just hope he doesn't want to mess with me."

"And the Wayfarers?" Sal asked.

"I'll be like you. I'll stay friendly."

Sal smiled. Then Tony got up and slammed a double over the manhole cover that was second base.

These concerns fell into the background as the school year continued. Squashed into his classroom with almost 80 other children, struggling with poor ventilation and little light, Tony thrived. It didn't matter that Miss McGowen followed the customary, mechanical lesson plan and that everything she taught had to be memorized. Tony wanted to learn, and he did.

Every morning began with the "Pledge of Allegiance." The boys and girls stood, held their hands over their hearts, and recited the words in front of the flag. Even though he didn't know what he was saying at first, Tony stood proudly with the others, chest puffed out, his hand in place. He knew what he was doing. Not only was he learning, he was learning to be an American.

With other subjects swirling around him and with nowhere to play at recess except a dark, damp, basement room, Tony focused on learning English. He had to know what people were saying to him. He had to know how to reply and how to begin a conversation himself.

Along with learning English came learning to read and write. If Tony was learning words and sentences in English, he had to learn to read and write them.

Every day, Tony memorized more words from his vocabulary book, but Miss McGowen liked to demonstrate the words as well. Teaching the English language, she strode to the back of the room. The sea of students parted so she could pass through.

"I open the door," she said opening it. "Tony Petrosino, what am I doing?"

Already she recognized Tony as a promising student.

"You are opening the door, Miss McGowen."

"Right."

Miss McGowen shut the door. "I shut the door," she said. "Tony, what have I done now?"

Again Tony gave the correct answer. He was proud and a little embarrassed by the extra attention.

"Now come up and do it yourself. Show the others."

This was even more embarrassing, but Tony did as he was told, trying hard not to look into the faces of his younger classmates. He hoped they were not resenting him.

Sometimes Tony's English lessons continued after school. He and Sal would meet on their steps at home. Sal was getting very good at English. He sounded out the words for Tony, and Tony pronounced them.

Bananas were becoming popular in the neighborhood. "Ba-na-na," Sal said.

"Banana," Tony replied.

They went on that day through other fruits and vegetables, which came in handy when Tony began to do the marketing for Mamma.

Mamma shopped for food every day because there was no way to preserve meat, fruit, or vegetables. What she bought depended on how much money there was. Mamma didn't mind the shopping so much. What she did mind was having to lug the heavy bags of groceries up those terrible narrow stairs.

There were too many and they scared her. They took

time away from her flower making, and the family needed the money. So Mamma felt relieved when Tony told her he'd take over the marketing.

All the children helped after school. Each day, the pile of carefully assembled artificial flowers grew and grew. But now Tony did less of that. Instead, he went shopping for his mamma.

Every afternoon, after he delivered the completed flowers to Alpha Flower, Tony went to Mario's for *liver* or *lamb shanks* or *sweet sausage*. He went to Angelo's for *mushrooms, broccoli, tomatoes,* or *peas*. He went to Veneto's for *bread* and to Cucina Italiano for pasta.

There didn't seem to be any English words for pasta. Linguini and tortellini stubbornly remained linguini and tortellini, and the catchall *noodles* didn't seem right. But everything else had its useful translation, and all these wonderful words were filling up Tony's vocabulary, even when he couldn't afford to fill up his stomach.

He started becoming known around Mulberry Street. People greeted him or smiled hello. Whenever Tony walked through the door, Mario the butcher—enormous in his stained white apron—wiped his hands, took off his glasses, and said in English, "So Tony, how are you misbehaving today?" It was their private joke. They both laughed.

With all these words and all these conversations, Tony was making great progress with his English. His reading and writing were improving too.

Miss McGowen taught reading by having her students

recognize and memorize individual words. "Boat," she would say, holding up a toy boat.

"Boat," the whole class would repeat. Then they would find the word in a passage in a book.

Tony found this way of learning boring, but he was good at it. He quickly found himself writing sentences and reading paragraphs and pages.

With other subjects, though, school was more like complete drudgery. In arithmetic, Miss McGowen made each student stand up and recite, "One times two equals two, two times two equals four, three times two equals six."

Nevertheless, Tony stayed with it. He was learning, he reminded himself, and that was the most important thing.

But even as he went on learning, Tony couldn't get the Ragpickers out of his head. He continued to take Vincenzo, Giuseppe, and Angelina to school, but he never got over being nervous about it. His brothers and sister liked school less than he did, but all the while he listened to their complaints about crowded classrooms and boring teachers, he was on the lookout for trouble.

He never waited on the Bayard Street corner again. Instead, he hung around inside the school or on the steps. But the Ragpickers were around and he knew it. He'd see them a distance away, lurking on a corner. He'd catch a smirk or a twist of the head from Harry Hickey, and know they were not through with him.

And then, of course, there were the Wayfarers. What would he do about them?

Chapter 5

Some weeks after the school year began, Mamma began doing garment work at home. She'd been talking with Mrs. Mirabelli in the hall. Mrs. Mirabelli took her by both elbows and said, "It is the season now. It is better. You will make more money."

Mrs. Mirabelli took Mamma back to her apartment. She pointed to a pile of coats and a pile of trousers. "Hand finishing," she said in Italian. "Fifteen cents a coat, ten cents a pair of pants."

"I can do that," Mamma said. "My mamma taught me how to sew. In Italy, I made most of our clothes."

Mamma went home. By suppertime, she was determined. "If we all help," she declared, "we will do better than with the flowers!"

Papà was half-asleep on the sofa, his hands folded on

his broad chest. "Good," he said, "good," and dozed off again.

Mrs. Mirabelli's garments came from Sidowski's on Hester Street. The next morning, Mamma was ready to go, but Tony convinced her to wait until after school. He would have marketing and flower making and schoolwork to do, but he didn't want her to go without him.

With the other children seated around the table and ready to begin their afternoon's labor, Tony helped Mamma down the dark stairs. Outside, Fabio the organ grinder was making his music. His monkey, dressed in red and tethered by a cord, was passing a hat.

On the street were the usual crowd of peddlers and passersby, ice cream vendors, and candy sellers.

"Chocolate covered cherries! Get your chocolate covered cherries! Two for a nickel! Only half a dime!"

Mamma shook her head. "So many people, so many people. Sometimes I think about the farm, Tonio."

Tony took her by the waist. "It's better here, Mamma. You know it is. We had nothing at the farm. It wasn't even ours."

Mamma sighed. "I know it. I get discouraged. I'll be fine."

Tony embraced her and patted her back. Slowly and carefully they made their way past all the people to the corner of Hester and Chrystie streets. Arriving, they climbed the two dusty flights of stairs to Sidowski's sweatshop.

They entered a dingy room, dimly lit by gas lamps.

The air was so thick with dust, it was difficult to breathe. In the middle of the room, at long rows of tables, women sat hunched over sewing machines. Dozens of skirts and dresses, along with men's vests, coats, and trousers were piled beside them on the floor. At the dirty windows at one end, and along the walls, sat women and bearded men doing the hand sewing.

Tony knew that many of these people were Jews. They lived on the Lower East Side, just like the Italians, only farther east. Tony didn't know any Jews. The only ones he'd seen were peddlers. He was intrigued by them and curious, but he kept his distance.

Mr. Sidowski was a large, bearded man. He came up and spoke to them. Tony's English was already so good he could interpret. Mamma went away with 10 coats for a start. She would sew the linings and finish the buttonholes. Tony had the chore of carrying all 10 home, his face barely visible behind the pile.

Now Mamma had to teach everyone to sew. Angelina and Giuseppe were naturals. They learned right away, but the older boys were hopeless from the start.

"Owww!" shouted Vincenzo, stabbing his finger with the needle for the sixth or seventh time. "I can't do this, Mamma. I'm no good at it."

"Shhh, Vincenzo, you'll be fine," Mamma said. "Just try it again. You'll see how easy it gets."

But it never got easy for Vincenzo—now quickly becoming Vinnie—or for Tony either. Tony just couldn't seem to get the needle through the fabric so it would make a perfect stitch. It kept coming out in the wrong place, or it stuck him in the finger, or it came out at an angle and just about ruined the lining. Worst of all, he couldn't even thread a needle properly. He found himself forever squinting at the eye and trying to poke the unwilling thread through.

Finally, a compromise was reached. Angelina and Giuseppe, on the verge of becoming Joey, would sew. Vinnie and Tony would carry the clothes back and forth to Sidowski's after school and continue with the artificial flowers.

Vinnie complained, but he did it. For Tony, it was perfectly fine. He was glad to carry the heavy coats and pants for Mamma. And to earn extra money, he'd begun delivering messages for Mario the butcher and Angelo the grocer to customers around Mulberry Street. For even more money, he was willing to make some of the hated artificial flowers when he had the time, though there wasn't ever much time. He was deep into his schoolwork now and loving it. Already it looked as if he might be moved up a grade.

Then in November, the weather turned. It grew cold, and the rain came down in buckets, washing the people away from Mulberry Street. The family had some warm clothing from the Old Country, but the children had grown out of most of it. The rest, threadbare as it was, just wasn't enough.

Tony always seemed to be cold. His fingers were always wet, and his feet squished in wet shoes. At school he sat with his arms crossed over his chest. At home the stove made a difference, and jumping into bed with his brothers helped generate some warmth.

Everyone came down with something. Angelina got a bad sore throat and chills and had to stay in bed. Mamma hovered over her but wouldn't call a doctor. They were too expensive and not trustworthy.

Fortunately, the little one was well in a week— jumping around, going back to school, and even getting back to her sewing. The family seemed to have turned a corner. Everyone's spirits improved. Then Papà lost his job.

They should have been expecting it. Construction work was always seasonal. No one would try to lay streets in the cold. But with so much else going on, the family hadn't planned ahead. And now there was Papà, slumped on the sofa, looking angry and helpless all at once.

Mamma tried to get him to help with the sewing. He was as good as Vinnie and Tony. She tried to get him to make artificial flowers, but he was as clumsy as before and couldn't seem to get the knack.

Mamma knew this had to change. Papà would have to get better at these things because without the pay from his construction job, they would need extra money to get through the winter. Papà kept trying, but he also began going out by himself in the evenings. He went to the poolrooms and saloons and came home a little drunk. He spent time playing cards with Luigi Mazzaferri and Luigi's friends.

Tony saw the hurt in Mamma's eyes when Papà would come in late smelling of beer. One night Papà was very late and very drunk. Tony had stayed up with Mamma, making more artificial flowers as she finished more buttonholes. Papà stumbled through the door, knocked over a pile of coats, and sprawled on the sofa.

At first he said nothing. Then, his speech slurred, he complained that Luigi's friend Gino had cheated him at poker.

Mamma got up from her chair. "You should not be playing poker with Luigi," she said.

There was silence. Italian wives did not speak to Italian husbands that way. Tony couldn't believe that Mamma had done it. He wondered what Papà would say.

Papà glared at Mamma from the sofa. "I have nothing else. I will play poker if I want to."

Mamma stood even taller. "You have a family, Pietro. You must help your family."

Papà glared some more but said nothing. The next night he went out, and the night after that. But each night, he came home early and sober. By the morning of the third day, he was at the table, trying once again to help make the flowers. Wrapping his huge, callused hands around a daisy, he was as likely to crush it as to shape it. But he was trying—trying and getting a little better.

Tony could see how hard it was for Papà. He was a strong man with a wife and children, reduced to making flowers. He kept on trying, but with so little success he began to get discouraged. Tony noticed that he began spending more time on the sofa, staring into space and clutching his hands. He began going out again, though not as much.

Tony remained as busy as before. Between school, homework, errands, marketing, making deliveries, and playing ball, there were hardly enough hours in the day. Each evening he fell asleep at once, even with Vinnie and Joey beside him.

Thanksgiving went by, and it got close to Christmas. Just before the winter break, Miss McGowen told Tony what he wanted to hear.

He was doing so well that in January, he would join a fourth-grade class! And he would probably move along more quickly after that. They were standing in the hall when Miss McGowen told him. He wanted to embrace her, but he was too embarrassed.

"Thank you," he said instead, "thank you, Miss McGowen."

Tony was so excited, he wanted to tell Mamma and Papà right away. But he had errands to run for Mario first. Then there was a game with Carl and Steve and Sal, and he couldn't be late for that.

Tony walked his sister and brothers home from school. He didn't want to tell them first because he didn't want them to feel less special. They were doing well enough in school, but not as well as he was. And Vinnie was having problems with his teacher. Vinnie was restless and headstrong. His teacher never seemed to have time for him except when there was a punishment to give for talking or not paying attention.

Tony knew exactly what he needed to buy for dinner. So as he dropped off his sister and brothers, he said, "Tell Mamma I'll be back in time to do the shopping."

Then he raced off.

But Mario had more errands than usual, and Tony *was* late for the game. The others wouldn't start without him, and the whole thing seemed to go on forever because no one could break a 7–7 tie until Sal hit a home run in the bottom of the 10th inning.

Tony didn't get back to Mulberry Street until it was almost dark. He bounded up the terrible stairs, ready with his apology and his good news.

Mamma was standing in the kitchen. "Vincenzo has disappeared."

"What?" Tony said in Italian. "How did it happen?"

The others were seated on the bed in the middle room, their heads hanging. Mamma explained that the two boys had decided to surprise Tony and do the marketing before he got back. Coming home, Vincenzo had suddenly darted down Grand Street. Papà had searched the neighborhood and found nothing—not a trace.

"I have an idea," Tony said.

He raced down the stairs. His own news would have to wait. He knew Vinnie had become friends with some newsboys who worked over on Broadway. He was sure that was where he had gone.

The stores on Grand Street were still open. Taking Broome would be quicker. Tony hurried across to

Broadway and started downtown. He passed Howard and crossed Canal, something he almost never did.

Like most of the immigrant community, Tony seldom left his neighborhood. The jobs, the shops, the *compaesani*—fellow Italians—were all there. The rest of the city wasn't very Italian and wasn't very nice to Italians, but Tony was speaking English now. He had guts and curiosity, and he had to find his brother.

Just below Canal, there was a crowd. Tony drew closer and saw a few newsboys, still carrying their papers, standing at the edge of a circle. Then he saw some Ragpickers and got scared.

He pushed his way through. In the middle of the circle, Harry Hickey was menacing Vinnie with a knife.

"Hey, wop!" Hickey was saying, holding out his other hand, "watcha got for me, wop?"

None of this made any sense. The Ragpickers, protective of their territory, were way outside it. And why would they go after a 10-year-old boy? He had nothing for them. Hickey and the others would know that.

It was insane. This had to be about Tony. The Ragpickers had seen him with Vinnie and realized they were brothers. They'd found Vinnie alone. Vinnie was a substitute for Tony.

Tony broke through the circle. "Hey, Hickey," he said in English, "don't you have the wrong Petrosino?"

Hickey whirled around. "Well, look who's here."

He took a step toward Tony, waving the knife. But before he could strike, what seemed like a wave crashed over them both. A dozen bodies rushed into the circle, and the Ragpickers were fighting for their lives.

Never at ease with fighting, Tony grabbed Vinnie and got out of the way. He was ready to flee the corner when he saw someone—only a blurred shape at that moment— go after Hickey.

Surprised, Hickey fell. The knife flew from his hand and landed several feet away. His attacker leaped onto his chest, straddled him, and punched away at his fleshy face.

Tony stood mesmerized. Vinnie tugged at his sleeve. "Tony, Tony, let's go."

But Tony couldn't leave. He couldn't help watching Hickey get beaten. He knew he shouldn't feel so glad, but he did.

The dark-haired boy on top of Hickey wasn't very big, and Hickey wasn't finished. He raised his arms to ward off the blows and with a huge effort sat up!

The others were still fighting, but in a moment, sensing that Hickey was rallying, they all stopped to watch. Hickey swatted the boy away as if he were a bug. He stood up, bent to retrieve his knife, and gestured with his hand. "Come on," he said to his followers, "we'll take care of these wops another time."

He looked straight at Tony. Then he was gone, surrounded by his ragtag gang.

Still glued to the spot, Tony watched them go. But as they disappeared up Broadway, he began to recognize the group that was left behind. He saw Paul and the boy with the mustache and peaked cap. It was the Wayfarers who had rescued him and Vinnie! Now he owed them a debt.

Standing in front of him was the boy who'd almost taken out Hickey. Even if he hadn't completely succeeded, he'd certainly saved the day.

The boy grabbed Tony by the shoulder. "Tonio," he said in broken English, "it's me, Tomasso."

Tony couldn't believe it. Tomasso from the ship—and he was a member of the Wayfarers!

"Tomasso! Thank you."

Tomasso smiled. "I couldn't let Hickey hurt my friend. I had to do something."

Paul was gathering the rest of the Wayfarers, but quickly Tony and Tomasso exchanged stories. Tomasso—now Tommy—was living with his parents on Prince Street. He was working as a bootblack and not going to school. He was learning English on the street. He'd joined the Wayfarers because they were there, because they were Italian, and because he wanted to belong. Tony should join too. Wouldn't it be great, the two of them together?

Tony smiled and shrugged, but the Wayfarers were going. Tomasso—Tommy— had to go too.

As they left, Tony caught a look from Paul. The look said, *Now that we've rescued you, isn't it time you came to your senses?*

Chapter 6

The sun was setting. Striding back up Broadway, Tony tried to get his brother to walk faster. "Everyone will be worried, Vinnie. It is very late."

But Vinnie didn't want to walk faster. He wanted Tony to listen to his fear. Still too tentative to use what English he'd learned, he spoke in Italian.

"I did nothing to him, Tony. He would have killed me for nothing."

"I know that, Vinnie. He wanted me. Today he would have settled for you."

"But, why?"

Tony tried to explain the unexplainable. How it all made no sense, how it was really just about being Italian and not Irish—or Irish and not Italian. Vinnie nodded. He was starting to understand.

But Tony seemed to understand less and less. Maybe he should join the Wayfarers after all. Maybe it was the safest way, the best way. The Wayfarers would protect him from the Ragpickers. He could be friends with Tomasso and be like him—quit school, get a full-time job, make more money, stop struggling with learning and a future he couldn't even understand. . . .

He stopped himself. He had to go to school. He didn't want to be a gang member—someone who fought all the time, did what the group decided, and had to leave a place when the leader said it was time to leave.

No, he had to keep going on his own, though he had to keep helping his family.

Tony and Vinnie walked several blocks in silence. Then Vinnie said, "I want to be a newsboy."

Tony stopped short and looked at him. "Vinnie, no. You must stay in school."

"I don't like school. You know I don't. All my friends are newsboys."

"But you don't want to be on the street. Don't you see? You'll get into trouble—"

"No, I won't. *You'll* see. And Papà will approve."

Tony knew that Vinnie was right. It made him wonder suddenly how Papà was going to react to the news of his school promotion.

He knew Papà disapproved of school. It made him suspicious.

"What are they doing at that school," he would say in Italian, "teaching you to disobey your papà?" And over and over, slumped on the sofa, he would say, "No child should be better than his parents."

Tony knew that this was a view from the world they had left. He also knew that his papà would never change. No one in Teggiano had ever gone to school. Why should his children go in America?

Papà didn't understand that America was different. In Teggiano, if you were one of the *contadini*, there was nowhere to go beyond your small rented farm. As a poor farmer, it didn't matter if you went to school or not. But in America, you could do anything. You didn't have to be stuck living the same hard life your parents lived, and it wasn't insulting not to want to.

Mamma was better about these things. When the subject of school came up, her eyes sparkled. "You go," she whispered to Tony when Papà left the room. "You go and do better."

Walking again in silence, Tony and Vinnie were almost home. They turned the corner onto Mulberry Street and squeezed through the crowd toward their building.

"Hey, Tony, how goes it?" shouted Marco the fruit peddler.

Tony waved. "Fine, fine, how are you?"

Then they were inside, Tony following Vinnie up the stairs, almost as if he were driving him. They reached the top and opened the door.

"Vinnie, you're safe!"

It was Angelina, but the whole family joined in,

hugging him, kissing him, welcoming him home.

"I was so scared," Mamma said. "Vincenzo, where were you?"

Vinnie glanced at Tony. *Say nothing about the fight, nothing about the gangs.*

"I was with the newsboys on Broadway," Vinnie said. "They're my friends. . . . Mamma, I want to be a newsboy."

In a second, Mamma's face seemed to go from relief to shock. "So soon, Vincenzo? You need to go to school. Your English isn't good yet. Helping here at home is enough."

Papà smiled. "This is a good idea, Mamma. He'll bring more money home."

Tony couldn't hold back any longer. "But school is important! Today Miss McGowen said I'll be moving ahead a grade in January!"

Somehow it hadn't come out right. It sounded more like a boast than a report, more like a criticism of Vinnie than a way of supporting his future.

But Mamma was ecstatic. "That's wonderful, Tonio. I'm so proud of you. Congratulations!"

Papà's face darkened. He looked away. "How very nice for you. Perhaps it's time for you to be a newsboy too."

Shattered, nearly in tears, Tony stared at his father. "Papà, my errands and my flower making, they bring in almost as much as a newsboy. And doing the marketing helps Mamma."

Papà nodded, only a little moved. Then there was a

discussion among Mamma, Papà, Vinnie, and Tony. In the middle of it, Tony could be heard shouting, "I will not leave school, I will not!"

Finally, they reached a compromise. It was determined, of course, by Papà but suggested by Mamma. Both boys would stay in school. But in the early-morning hours, both would be part-time newsboys.

"Oh, Mamma, do I have to?" Vinnie wailed when it was clear that school remained in his future.

"*Si*," Mamma said, nodding, "*Si*, Vincenzo."

Papà didn't say a word.

Meanwhile, Tony was thinking about the lack of sleep, the errands he wouldn't run, and the baseball games he couldn't play if he was going to get his schoolwork done. "We'll go to Publisher's Row tomorrow morning," he said, sounding knowledgeable and confident, but feeling nothing but fear and loss.

Now he had to find Sal—Sal, the part-time newsboy, the one who had told him on his very first day in America that selling newspapers was a good idea. Sal had told him about Publisher's Row, where the big newspapers had their offices, but he hadn't told him much more. Now Sal would tell him the rest.

"I'm going down to Sal's," Tony said and ran out of the apartment.

The stairs seemed to moan beneath his feet as he sped down them. Something would be changing now. Something would be different. He banged on Sal's door, but Sal wasn't home. Mrs. Amalfi wasn't sure when he'd

be in or whether he'd be selling papers tomorrow
morning.

Trouble. He'd have to pull this together himself.

He remembered Sal saying something about the *New
York Tribune*. That sounded like a good place to try. Sal
had said that they charged you five cents for ten papers
and you got to sell them for a penny apiece. Not a bad
profit if you sold a lot, but you had to start off with a
stake—some money that would buy you papers before
you sold any.

Under the circumstances, Tony had no qualms about
borrowing from Mamma. When he asked her, though, he
felt nervous. Money was always so tight. How could he
ever ask for any?

Mamma smiled, gave him twenty cents, and patted his
hand.

That was encouraging at least, but all night long, Tony
tossed and turned in bed. He'd be leaving the
neighborhood constantly now, selling newspapers to
people he didn't know. Many of them wouldn't even be
Italian. Some, like Miss McGowen, might even be Irish!
Vinnie had no idea what he was getting into. He just
thought it would be more fun than school.

Finally, Tony dropped off to sleep. In what seemed
like minutes later, he was being shaken awake! Groggy
and exhausted, he looked up into the face of his papà.

Pietro was no longer working uptown, but he still rose
at five-thirty every morning. Just the right time to rout
his two older sons out of bed.

Vinnie was sleepy. He didn't want to get up. "It's too early, Papà," he groaned, curling into a ball.

Great, thought Tony. *Vinnie brought this on us both. Now he's the one who doesn't want to go.*

Papà shook Vinnie again. "Vincenzo, it's time."

Vinnie knew better than to disobey. "*Sì*, Papà."

He rolled onto the floor. Tony rolled after him.

Mamma was already bustling in the kitchen, preparing a breakfast of rolls, milk, and coffee. Pulling on clothes, splashing their faces with water from the sink, Tony and Vinnie got ready. In half an hour, they were outside.

The sun was just beginning to come up on a cold, gray winter day. Mulberry Street was waking up, preparing for the customary invasion of people. There was a pushcart peddler here, a wagon there. The stores were not yet open but beginning to set shoes or underwear out on the street in bins. Most of the produce stayed indoors. It was too cold to leave perishable food outside.

Tony tightened his scarf and adjusted Vinnie's as they started downtown. The wind pierced his jacket and he shivered. Vinnie seemed all right, but maybe this wasn't the best day for a beginning.

Tony guided them over to Mott Street. They could follow it down to Chatham Square and pick up Park Row, which turned into Publisher's Row south of City Hall Park. It was the most convenient route. It was also one block east of Mulberry Street and just far enough away to avoid Mulberry Bend.

On Mott Street in the early morning, there were

drunks sprawled on stoops and clusters of homeless boys—most dressed in rags and some without shoes— huddled together in doorways or on heating grates, seeking what warmth they could find. Eyes cast downward, Tony and Vinnie passed by.

Then they crossed Canal Street and found themselves on the part of Mott that was the main street of Chinatown. Looking around, they saw strange food markets and curio stores, a restaurant called the Port Arthur, Chinese men with pigtails, and a church. Compared to their bustling neighborhood, Chinatown was oddly quiet. The boys were curious, fascinated, and uncertain. But Tony hurried them on. There was no time to lose.

Tony knew that the *Tribune* was on the corner of Nassau and Spruce. Reaching City Hall Park, passing the entrance to the Brooklyn Bridge, discovering *The New York Times* and Publisher's Row, it didn't take long to find the building they wanted.

A guard directed them to the *Tribune* distribution room. It was huge and full of boys. Most were lined up at a desk, where an assistant circulation manager was handing out piles of newspapers in exchange for money. Others—more of the homeless boys Tony and Vinnie had seen on Mott Street—were draped around pillars and a coal stove, sleeping.

Tony noticed that most of the older boys, the ones who seemed to have more experience, were up at the front of the line. The littler ones—even a girl or two—hung back and waited their turn. Tony made sure he and Vinnie went right to the end of the line. He didn't want to step on anyone's toes that first day.

It didn't take long to reach the desk. With his bowler hat pushed back on his head, the assistant circulation manager regarded them sternly. "Twenty papers please, sir," Tony said, handing him a dime. He wanted to see how things went before spending all their money.

The man handed him the papers and looked immediately at the next boy. Tony gave Vinnie half the copies and got them out of there.

But where were they going to go? Newsboys seemed everywhere, hawking papers on every corner. Where was a spot for them?

Across the street, at the very tip of City Hall Park, seemed a good place to try. It was conspicuous. A lot of people came past.

"What do you think?" Tony asked Vinnie.

Vinnie was so thrilled to be a newsboy—but so terrified at actually becoming one—that all he could do was nod. They crossed the street and set up shop. Tony faced in one direction. Vinnie faced the other.

"Get your early morning *Tribune!*" Tony shouted.

Vinnie tried to do the same but not as loudly.

Nothing happened. Then a man walked by. He looked like a well-dressed businessman. Pointing, he said, "I'll have one of those."

Quickly Tony folded the paper and presented it.

"Thank you," the man said, pulling out a nickel. "Keep the change."

"Thank *you*, sir," Tony said, staring at the coin. He couldn't believe his good fortune. He'd sold one paper and already made four-and-a-half cents. Was this going to be that easy?

Suddenly his feet went flying from under him. He landed hard on the ground, elbows first. He heard Vinnie yell. Vinnie had been tackled too.

Tony sat up—and saw a boy standing over him. He was a skinny boy with tangled blond hair.

"You're on my corner," the boy said. "You don't want to do that."

Chapter 7

"Nope," said another boy. He was shorter and heavier than the blond boy, and he had dark hair. "You don't want to do that."

He was the one who had tackled Vinnie.

"I'm sorry," Tony said. "I didn't know."

"You should have found out," said the blond boy, folding his arms. "Nobody takes somebody else's corner. Newsboy code."

"I see," Tony said, wishing all the while that he'd been able to find Sal. Sal would have told him about this. "It won't happen again, I promise."

A moment passed. No one seemed to know what to do next.

"So, are you gonna move on outta here?" the blond boy asked, though it was really a command.

"Sure," Tony said, "don't worry."

He got to his feet. He had to think fast. "Look, we're sorry we got in your way. It's our first day doing this. Could you tell us what we can and can't do? We'd be grateful."

The mood changed. "So it's your first day," the blond boy said. "Well, that explains a lot." He smiled and helped Vinnie up. "We've got to sell papers, but when I can, I'll fill you in. You didn't look like the sort who'd get in someone's way."

Tony remembered Harry Hickey's threat at their first meeting: *Don't you ever do nothin' that gets in our way, you hear?* He shuddered. "No, no, we're not," he said.

They introduced themselves. The blond boy was Alfie, and the dark-haired one was Buzz. They'd been newsboys for a year or more, mostly together. They had run away from really poor homes and would never go back, slept mostly on the street or at a newsboy lodging house. There was a good lodging house up at Duane and Chambers, with really clean beds and good food. But they wouldn't stay in that kind of place for long. Too many rules.

A customer came by, a tall man in a dark suit. Buzz stood out of the way, hiding the stack of papers. Alfie, looking as friendly as he could, stepped forward, grinning.

"Please, sir, my last paper. Only a penny. Just one cent. Then I can go home, sir."

He waved the copy of the *Tribune*.

The man stopped. "Well, why not? I'll be glad to help you out, young man. Here's your penny."

He placed the coin in Alfie's outstretched palm, plucked the paper from his other hand, and was on his way.

Alfie danced around, waving the penny. Another "last" paper quickly took the place of the one just sold. The game began again.

Tony and Vinnie looked at each other. They had learned a trick of the trade.

"You two, you'd do it even better," Buzz said. "You put the little one out front. He looks cute and friendly. The customers eat it up."

"I like that," said Tony, "but what about tips?"

He was remembering his own incredible luck first time out.

"They're an accident mostly," Alfie said. "Some of the boys do magic tricks or sing or something, but I don't believe in that. There is something I call 'the little influencer' though. I'll show you in a minute."

He sold a couple more papers. Then a man came by with a nickel.

Alfie searched his pockets. "Sorry, sir, no change."

"Never mind, don't bother about it," said the man, tucking the paper under his arm and walking off.

Alfie whirled around, grinning more broadly than before. "See, it worked. Doesn't always though. Sometimes they make you go get the change if you can't produce it."

"What if you can't find any?" Vinnie asked.

"Then you take a long time and hope the creep

doesn't wait. If he does, you hope he'll let you off the hook."

Tony wasn't so sure about the "influencer," but he was learning fast about the ways of newsboys. Maybe it was time they went off on their own, though. They had papers to sell too.

But there was still the crucial question. "Alfie," Tony said, "if all the good corners are already taken, where can we sell our papers?"

Alfie shrugged, sold another *Trib*, took out a cigarette butt, and lit it. "Most of the good spots, the best corners, you gotta buy from the owner. Some kid who gets sick or wants out of the business."

"But we don't know anyone," Tony said, "and we don't have any money."

Alfie grinned again, squatted on his haunches, and poked out the butt. "There's a good spot up at Chatham Square where the elevated trains come together. Lots of good traffic. Kid who had it disappeared a few days ago. No one knows how, and no one's asking. He was sort of rough, nobody's favorite. Yesterday—still nobody there. You might have a shot if he doesn't come back."

"We're going," said Tony. "Thanks a lot. See you tomorrow at the *Trib*, if we luck out."

"We'll be there," said Alfie.

"Nowhere else to be," said Buzz.

Tony would have loved hanging out with these boys awhile longer. They were easier company than a lot of the boys at school or in the neighborhood. They were more comfortable with themselves and the world. But now they had to get to Chatham Square.

Even chillier now in the early-morning cold, Tony hurried Vinnie back the way they had come such a short time ago. Clutching their papers, hustling, they could see their breath hanging in the air like smoke.

Mounted on huge, thick, iron supports, the tracks of the Second and Third Avenue elevated trains—known to everyone as two of the Els—converged at Chatham Square. A large iron canopy spread over them. Blocks away the canopy loomed, a perfect place to sell newspapers. In lousy weather, it offered protection. During the rush hour, which was fast approaching, people would be flooding on and off the trains—the perfect collection of customers.

Tony and Vinnie were getting closer. Finally they were there. To one side, a boy was already set up. On the other side, by some miracle, there was no one.

Quickly, Tony and Vinnie went into action. Vinnie flaunted his "last paper" in an Italian accent, while Tony hung behind him with the stack. Some passengers came and went. No one bought. No one even paid attention. Then Vinnie got down on one knee and spread his arms. He held a *Trib* in one hand. Minutes later, he had his first sale.

The crowds kept coming now from both directions. Vinnie kept smiling, kneeling, and selling papers, and Tony kept feeding him more. They were too scared to try the "influencer" yet. That would have to come later. But keeping their ears open, they heard the boy on the other side shouting the headlines. That seemed like a good ploy. They tried it and sold more papers.

In less than an hour, they *were* down to their last one!

"We'd better get more papers," Tony said. "There's still time before school."

The *Tribune* offices were several blocks away, but the boys hurried down. Using their profits, they bought 40 more papers and hurried back. Would another newsboy be standing in their spot when they appeared? Would they have to challenge him? Would it be the kid whose spot it was before?

As they reached Pearl Street and could see the iron canopy up ahead, they walked faster. A boy in a cap was crossing the street, entering the station area. He carried no newspapers, but his partner could have brought them there ahead of him.

"Oh, no!" gasped Vinnie. "We can't lose it already!"

He and Tony were running now. They dashed into the station. No one was at the spot. The boy had been going to the train after all!

The two brothers stopped where they were and hugged. Then they set up shop again and sold more papers.

When Vinnie got tired of being the front man, Tony got to try again. His first time out, he got down on one knee, flourished the paper, and sold! He wasn't as little and cute as Vinnie, but he was still sympathetic and winning. Besides, people were going to work. They wanted the morning paper.

There weren't any more unexpected tips, though. That very first one—that first-time lucky—was all they got that day.

"Tony," said Vinnie in a whisper, "we only have three papers left!"

"It's all right," said Tony. "We have to go soon."

He asked his next customer the time. Twenty minutes to nine. They had to leave for school. In moments, the last papers were gone.

"How much money did we make?" asked Vinnie as Tony hurried him along. Their noses were tingling, their fingers frozen in their worn-out gloves.

"Sold 60 papers, made 30 cents, plus the extra 4 cents from my tip," Tony replied.

"Do we get to keep some of it?"

"This is for the family," Tony said. "It goes to Mamma. She can decide."

They reached school. Joey had been appointed to bring Angelina by himself, and Tony didn't see Vinnie for the rest of the day. But as they walked home afterwards Vinnie kept asking, "How much do you think she'll give us?"

Mamma hugged them both when they came through the door. "The two of you look very pleased with yourselves," she said, laughing that little laugh she reserved for special occasions.

Tony told the story of their morning—of their meeting with Alfie and Buzz, of Chatham Square. Then he gave Mamma the money.

Mamma handed each of them a penny. "For doing so well," she said.

She gave the rest back to Tony. "You'll need this to buy more papers. You're already so good, you'll sell even more tomorrow."

Vinnie looked pleased and disappointed all at once. Tony had to smile. Mamma didn't have an education, but she certainly knew how to look out for her family.

Chapter 8

The next morning, Papà didn't even have to wake them. They were up at dawn, long before he was. Mamma got them breakfast and dressed them as warmly as she could. Then they were out and down the stairs in a flash.

It was still dark, but that didn't matter. They made a beeline for the *Tribune* distribution room.

Arriving so early, they found a lot more sleepers than the day before, but already the line was forming at the assistant circulation manager's desk.

Alfie and Buzz were a few boys ahead of them. They shook hands all around.

"How'd it go?" Alfie asked.

"We got the spot," Tony said. "No one was there."

"Good. I thought you'd get it if you were quick."

"Nobody quicker," grinned Tony.

Alfie looked away. "They found the kid in the river."

"They did?" said Tony and Vinnie together.

"Yeah, foul play," said Buzz.

"Do they know what happened?" asked Tony.

"Probably the Ragpickers, one of them gangs. They're always up to no good," said Alfie.

Tony wondered. Would the Ragpickers be coming for him in Chatham Square now? Would they take care of him the way they'd taken care of this other kid? He forced the thought out of his mind.

"Good luck today," Alfie said, giving Tony and Vinnie the thumbs-up.

"Same to you," said Tony, adding a thumbs-up of his own.

They bought 50 papers—all they could carry—and they sold them. They bought 40 more and sold those too. With a couple of tips thrown in, they came away with a 50-cent profit.

Tony was so excited he almost neglected school for the day. Mamma was happy too. This time she put away some of the money. "It will help us have a Christmas," she said.

So every morning now, Tony and Vinnie launched themselves out of bed, wolfed down their breakfasts, got their papers, and sped off to Chatham Square. Pretty soon it became known on the street that the spot under the Els was their spot for the early-morning hours, and no one tried to take it. Business got better too. They were up to 95 papers a day. And every so often, they got to see a few of Vinnie's newsboy friends or steal a moment for coffee with Alfie and Buzz.

Alfie snorted when Tony asked him about his past. "We don't have no past. Don't have no future neither. We grew up in Five Points, Buzz and me."

Tony's eyes widened. Five Points was at the southern tip of Mulberry Bend—the worst place in the city before the Bend took over the honor.

"My dad was always boozed up," Alfie continued, "Mom had to take in washin' till she died of consumption. Every day I'd come home, Dad would be ready with the belt. I had to get outta there somethin' fierce."

All the while, Buzz was sipping his coffee and nodding. "Yeah," he said, "my story ain't no better. Both parents dead of drink. Sister up to no good. No way to pay the rent on a basement room. The street's the better life, I'll tell ya."

"It's awful hard in the winter though," Alfie added.

"I'd bet on it," said Tony. "I get cold just trying to sell my papers."

The very thought of living on the street in winter made him yank his scarf tighter. Here were boys who had grown up worse than he had. They were living worse than he was even though his family was poor.

Knowing this helped a little when, with Christmas upon them, things took another turn for the worse.

Sidowski's laid off all their home workers.

"Merry Christmas," Tony thought when Mamma came home with the news, her face downcast, her voice a whisper. But of course, the home workers weren't the only ones who had been laid off. The season had ended; the clothes for spring and summer had all been made and shipped. Full employment wouldn't be needed until March or April, when it would be time to make garments for fall and winter. Many of the shop workers had been laid off too.

Of course the family had known this would happen, but it was their first year in America. Just as it had been with Papà's job, they hadn't planned ahead.

There was a flurry of activity. Mamma brought in more boxes of flowers, and everyone had to pitch in to assemble them. Even Tony—selling his papers, running his errands, doing the marketing and his schoolwork—sat down in the evening and pasted petals.

He had a little more time in the winter, since there wasn't much opportunity for baseball. But it was the newspaper business that was making the difference. He and Vinnie were earning more than three dollars a week! That was more than the ten-dollar monthly rent.

Those three dollars were especially important because Papà was still not doing very much. Sometimes he sat at the table, struggling painfully to make the flowers. Sometimes he sat in the corner, folding and unfolding his massive arms. With everyone so crowded together, with the air so stale and the light so poor, one disgruntled person made everyone else more cramped, more bored, more unhappy. Tony wished spring would come just to relieve the tension in the room.

But first there had to be Christmas. Mamma had said there would be one, and there was. The newsboy earnings contributed to that as well. Mamma had said they would help, and they did.

The Petrosinos couldn't afford the baubles in the shop windows on Grand and Mulberry Streets, but Tony, Vinnie, Joey, and Angelina got candy from the Napoli on Christmas morning. Tony got a special supply of Jujyfruits. Vinnie was delighted with his Red Hot Dollars.

They didn't go to Mass because they seldom went to Mass. The Church of the Transfiguration was all Irish, and Mamma didn't like the smug Italian priest who performed the services for Italians in the basement. What they did have was Christmas dinner, in the middle of the day, with Luigi Mazzaferri as an invited guest.

"*Mammamia*, I can't wait!" Luigi declared as everyone watched Mamma finish preparing the food.

Tony rolled his eyes and looked away.

But then Mamma opened the oven door, and out came the lasagna and the manicotti, perfectly baked and smelling of ricotta and mozzarella and tangy tomato. There were breads and vegetables and a bottle of cheap Chianti too. Everyone sighed and dug in. For a few minutes at least, this small, airless room was quieter than Tony could ever remember.

When everyone had finished, there was the final course: irresistible cannolis from Mantegna's Bakery. Afterward, everyone sat stupefied until Papà suggested a walk around the neighborhood. Then they raised themselves and set out, greeting the Mirabellis, the Paccis, the Amalfis, and other families, all of them sharing the same walk.

Tony was especially glad to see Sal. They had finally talked about being newsboys—by then Tony had mastered most of the fine points. But in the last few weeks, Tony had been so busy, they'd hardly seen each other. Besides, Sal was selling his papers over on Chambers Street and doing most of it in the afternoon, which made getting together even less possible.

"Hope I'll see more of you in the new year," Sal said.

"I hope so too," Tony replied, wondering at the same time what had happened to Tomasso. He hadn't seen him or the Wayfarers since the Ragpickers fight.

But then there was New Year's, with noisemakers and a lot of carrying on. A new year in America—their *first* new year in America! And after that was the relentless round of the year to come.

The dark days of winter melted into spring, and with spring, the tempo of everything accelerated and everyone's mood improved. The days got longer, the sun shone brighter, and Papà went back to work laying streets.

No longer stranded in the house, Pietro Petrosino was a different person—friendlier, more sympathetic and loving. He still came home late sometimes, but remembering Mamma's anger, he was never drunk. Mamma went back to doing her garment work, exhausting and dreary as it was. The children went on making artificial flowers. Tony did his errands and marketing, and he and Vinnie went on selling their newspapers.

There was more money now. It was never enough, but

at least they could feel they wouldn't starve or be put out on the street. And although Vinnie was still floundering at school, Joey and Angelina were doing well and Tony was doing even better. Studying his English and arithmetic, learning about history and local politics and patriotism, by June he had passed a test that would put him in seventh grade the following fall.

Tony was proud. Now he could pledge allegiance to the flag and know what all the words meant. Mamma was proud too, and so was Sal. He'd be going into eighth grade in the fall. By the end of the school year, maybe he and Tony would be in the same class!

Chapter 9

Soon after Tony took the test for school, the Wayfarers reappeared. He was coming home with his brothers and sister, and there they were, waiting in two rows.

Tony knew this was a test of courage. You walked between the rows, and everybody hit you. He knew he couldn't run away. They would go after him and beat him anyway. Quickly he told Vinnie, Joey, and Angelina to go home. Then he walked over to meet his fate.

He smiled at the Wayfarers standing there, ducked his head, and plowed through. Ready for the blows, expecting them, he was surprised to feel no pain. He had run through the Wayfarers untouched.

Confused, he turned around. The boys still stood there, scowling. Paul walked up to him and took him by the shirt. "This wasn't everyone's wish," he said, "but I'm givin' you another chance."

73

"Thanks," said Tony, gasping, "how generous of you."

"Don't mock me, boy. Will you join us now?"

Paul released Tony's shirt. Slowly Tony shook his head. He knew he was making life harder for himself. He didn't want to insult anyone, had no idea what the Wayfarers would do to him next.

"I'm sorry," he said over and over, "I'm sorry."

The Wayfarers were gone. Mulberry Street crowded around him. Only Tomasso remained.

"Tony, I want to be friends with you."

"So," said Tony, "be friends."

"I can't. You know why."

"Does the gang tell you everything you can do, Tomasso? When to get up, when to eat, when to go to the bathroom?"

"No, no, that's not fair. But the gang has rules and wishes. I am a member. I must accept—"

"Then do it, Tomasso, do it. But don't expect me to. I cannot join."

"Then we will not be friends."

"It seems not."

Tomasso—Tommy—embraced him. Then he too was gone, leaving Tony sad and bewildered and standing in the middle of a sunny, boisterous, Mulberry Street afternoon, remembering those good times on the ship.

Strangely, Tony's bewilderment only increased. For some reason, his holdout, his continual rejection of the Wayfarers, had gained him respect. Had his hard-headed determination been interpreted as admirable? Or had the Wayfarers just run out of energy?

Whatever the reason, when any of the gang saw him now, they were actually friendly. Nothing more than a nod or a smile, but that was better than hostility. For the time being, it was one less thing that Tony had to worry about.

Soon it was summer. The air was swollen with humidity, and the sun beat down on too many people crowded into too many small spaces. Papà came home soaked with sweat from a day on the streets. Half-moons of perspiration formed in Mamma's armpits, and beads of it clung to her forehead. All the children complained about being stuck in the sweltering tenement apartment when they wanted to be outside.

"Mamma," said Joey, "please. They've opened a hydrant on Elizabeth Street. I want to go."

"Two dozen more flowers, then you go," Mamma said, bending to her own work, knowing how heartless she sounded, yet knowing they needed the money.

Now that school was out, Tony and Vinnie were spending longer mornings selling papers at Chatham Square. Someone else had the spot in the afternoons— they never hung around to find out who—but that was all right. Tony still had all his errands to run and the marketing to do, and the occasional baseball game still stole some of his time. Vinnie had become a part-time messenger for the Stabile Bank at the corner of Mulberry and Grand.

But for Tony, that summer was a summer of friendship more than anything else. Not with Alfie or

Buzz or Tomasso, but with Sal—who had wanted to see more of him in the new year.

In the evenings, when Tony could break out of the cauldron that was Apartment 5C, he would meet Sal and they would go exploring. Older now, they prowled the candy stores and cafés, stopping here or there for a soda or an espresso or a slice of ricotta cheesecake. They used the money they'd been allowed from their newsboy earnings and other jobs. Then they would return home and scramble up the stairs to the roof, where they knew their families would be waiting.

On those hot summer nights, no one could sleep in their tenement apartments. The rooms were sweltering, and the few windows were no help at all unless you slept right under them. If you could, you moved to the roof, carrying mattresses, bedding, anything that might make you more comfortable.

The Petrosinos and the Amalfis were always among the first, even though the Amalfis had to come all the way from the second floor. They had their special places, their special family corners. With three children, the Amalfis needed almost as much space as the Petrosinos. But after some weeks, the families blended together. Nights under the stars became nights with a common cause.

Often, Tony and Sal found themselves their own corner. They sprawled against the railing and gazed up at the starry sky, surrounded by fire escapes and water towers.

One night, Sal said, "That song we heard in the café, what did it remind you of?"

"Italy," said Tony. "It seems so far away, so long ago."

"I could never go back," said Sal.

"Me either," said Tony.

"In Italy I was a part of the earth, not even a person. Here I am a person."

Tony laughed. "Among many other persons."

"Yes," said Sal, "but I know who I am."

So do I, thought Tony. *So do I . . . I hope, I hope, I hope.* And many was the night that summer, baking in the heat talking with Sal, that Tony would hear that voice inside himself again: *I hope, I hope, I hope.*

But then he had to go back to school, and in a moment, it seemed, the winter was upon them once more. Papà lost his job again and sat at home making everyone miserable again. Mamma lost the garment work as well, so everyone had to make more flowers.

Tony tried to sell more papers, but there was only so much he could do. *Would it always be like this?* he wondered. *Would there always be this endless cycle, this round of desperation when the work dried up and the cold came on and there was no relief until spring?*

And just in case Tony was interested in forgetting them, the Ragpickers came along with a little reminder.

He and Vinnie were at Chatham Square on a cold winter morning in January. They were blowing on their hands and stamping the pavement to try and keep their feet warm. Gradually their pile of papers was shrinking. Then from across the street, Tony heard, "Hey, wop, wop, wop! Hey, wop!"

He looked over. There was a bunch of Ragpickers slouching close together, their black clothing etched against the ice gray of the morning.

Why me? Tony wanted to know. Even as he asked the question, he knew there was no answer.

And now, almost in slow motion, they were crossing the street.

Quickly Tony sold another paper. Then another.

"Vinnie," he said, "get out of here. I'll catch up with you later."

Vinnie saw the Ragpickers coming. "Tony, let me stay."

"No, please go. This is my fight, whatever it is."

Vinnie went, looking over his shoulder.

So here was Hickey once again, surrounded by his lieutenants and looking for some impossible satisfaction.

Tony looked at him and his posturing gang members. He knew he was pretty safe in this crowded area.

"I want a paper," Hickey said.

A *paper?* Tony wondered. There were a few left, so he handed one over and waited for the response.

Hickey stuck the *Tribune* under his arm. "Here's your penny, wop!" he said, throwing the coin on the ground.

Tony stopped it under his shoe. Hickey marched off, his cohorts swaggering behind him.

Tony watched them go. At the very least, wouldn't Hickey have stolen the paper?

Tony picked up the coin. So this was just another warning over nothing. Would they ever end? Would they end the way they did for the boy in the river? Tony had to live with the fear.

Meanwhile, on March 18, he got to celebrate his 14th birthday. Like any boy in America, he had a chocolate cake with chocolate icing. Mamma made it for him, and he loved it. Then in June, Tony and Sal graduated from eighth grade.

When Tony's teacher, Miss O'Brien, announced that he had passed, he couldn't believe it. He knew he had tried very hard. He really hadn't thought he'd succeed. Sal gave him an elbow in the ribs to convince him. Tony gave Sal an elbow back.

As he was leaving school, Tony ran into Miss O'Brien. She shook his hand and said, "You know, Tony, not too many boys have come so far as quickly as you have."

Tony smiled.

"I hope you will be able to do something more with your education," she continued. "Just because you *can* leave school now doesn't mean you should."

As Tony listened to Miss O'Brien, he engraved her words in his memory. Could she help him continue his education, he wondered?

She didn't say. He was afraid to ask. The moment slipped by. She began talking to someone else. Tony left, found his brothers and sister, and told them he had passed.

"I guess that means you can stop going to school," Vinnie said.

Tony knew where the question was leading and wouldn't go there. "Yes, Vinnie, it does," he said sadly.

When he got home, Tony told Mamma about graduating and what Miss O'Brien had said. Mamma was thrilled. "*Magnifico*, Tonio, but if you could continue, how would you do it?"

"I don't know, Mamma. There are technical schools. The aid societies have classes."

"And what about your papà?"

Tony opened his mouth. He knew what his papà would say. He didn't want to hear it.

He mentioned nothing for a few weeks. Then there was a graduation ceremony with local officials, the American flag onstage, diplomas, and patriotic music. Everyone got to march up to the podium and shake hands with the principal.

When Tony came off the stage with his diploma, he felt like a king. When he sang " The Star-Spangled Banner," he felt almost like a real American. He and Sal shook hands outside the school. They might even belong in this new world now.

It was the right time to talk with his father. Tony waited through dinner that night. It was too crowded at the table, with everyone eating and talking. Afterward, the family drifted to other rooms before sitting down to an evening of flower making. Everyone except Papà, who remained in his chair.

Tony sat opposite him. "Papà, today I graduated from eighth grade."

Papà looked up. His eyes narrowed. "Excellent," he said in Italian, "now you can go to work all the time."

Already Tony was losing ground. "But Papà, that isn't what I want. My teachers . . . they think . . . more education—"

"Enough with education, Tonio. Now you will do like me. You will work. You will be a full-time newsboy."

"But I have been a newsboy, Papà. It will not help me—"

"It will help the family, Tonio. That is good enough."

"But I help the family, Papà. I do more than anyone!" He stood up. "It is foolish not to—"

"What?" said Papà, reddening. "You call me a fool? Your own Papà? Enough! You must give more to the family!"

Tony's heart pounded. "No!" he shouted and ran for the door.

As he turned the knob, he looked back, saw his father's blazing eyes and the turning away. Then he was gone down the stairs.

Chapter 10

Tony had been sitting on the front steps for hours. He'd been looking out at the cafés and the customers and listening to the murmur of the voices, the clinking of the glasses and coffee cups, on Mulberry Street. People together, families together—everyone sharing this hot, early summer, June night.

America told him he could go farther, do more, but where could he go and what could he do without Papà's approval? Without that, he had no family. Without his family, he had no one.

Papà had brought him here. In return, Tony owed him respect and loyalty and love without conditions. No matter how much he felt that things should be different, he had to help his family.

He sighed deeply and took one last look at the bright

and boundless Mulberry Street night. He was an Italian boy, the son of an Italian from Teggiano. He had no choice. He would listen to his father.

But would Papà even talk to him now? Had he swept himself out of the family by his rudeness and disrespect?

Slowly Tony began to climb the stairs. They were longer, darker, and worse-smelling than they had ever been. Before, he had run up and down those stairs with abandon. Now, at each landing he had to stop and catch his breath.

When he finally reached the fifth floor and his apartment, he was exhausted. He was also afraid.

If his father did not take him back, he would have nowhere to go. He would be like Alfie and Buzz—alone, abandoned, a street kid with nothing . . .

Tony threw open the door.

Papà was still sitting at the kitchen table, in the same place he'd been sitting when Tony stormed out. But now he was facing the table, his broad back in the white undershirt visible from the door. The others sat around him. As if nothing had happened, they were making their quota of artificial flowers.

"Papà, I'm sorry!" Tony yelled.

Papà stood up, scraping his chair on the floor. He turned around. Expressionless, he looked at Tony, standing in the middle of the room.

Tony couldn't tell what his father was feeling. "Papà, I should have listened. I'll be a newsboy. Everything will be good."

83

He fell on his knees.

In a moment his papà was on the floor beside him, taking him in his huge arms and saying, "It's all right, Tonio. You are forgiven. We are together now."

And then everyone really was together again. Tony hugged Mamma and Vinnie, Joey and Angelina, and they all sat down together to finish the artificial flowers.

A little later, though, when things seemed calmer, Tony was surprised to discover that some changes had been made.

Mamma looked up from a large purple rose. "Tony," she said, "while you were gone, we talked as a family."

Vincenzo didn't want to continue with school. He wanted to work full-time as a messenger for the Stabile Bank. They liked him there, and the pay was good. He would say he was 14, not 12, and no one would know. The school was so crowded, he would not be missed. Giuseppe would do the marketing, and he and Angelina would continue working with Mamma after school and in the summer. And now that Tony would be a full-time newsboy and Papà had forgiven him, he would have no partner after next week.

Mamma looked sad when she said this. Who knew better than she how much Tony wanted to continue his education?

Tony smiled. After everything that had gone on this evening, after all the conversations he'd had with Vinnie, there was no point in bringing up the subject of school. All he could say instead was, "Vinnie was the one who wanted to be a newsboy."

84

"Why don't you ask Salvatore to join you?" Papà said. "I was playing cards with his papà last week. The boy likes the work. Together, you will help each other."

Was there something funny going on here, some pre-arranged plan? Tony didn't think so. Anyway, it seemed a nice idea—working with Sal and seeing him every day. But even as he thought about it, he wondered all over again: Why were they going to be newsboys? Shouldn't they be doing something else?

In bed that night, it was hard to relax. Tony watched the shadows on the ceiling, wondering if he'd done the right thing. But of course he had. There was no other way.

The next afternoon, he caught up with Sal at the Napoli. Signor Benevento, the proprietor, had recently installed a spun-sugar sculpture of Mount Vesuvius in the window. It was all purple and gold. The volcano itself was erupting. Sal was sitting at a table staring at it when Tony came in.

"Is that the most ridiculous thing you've ever seen?" Tony asked.

"I think so," Sal replied. "But I was remembering the first time I brought you here, on your first night in America."

"I would have loved it then," said Tony.

"I might have loved it myself," Sal agreed.

"Are we so hard to please now?"

"No. We just know what's out there now. We know what we can have."

"Tell that to my father," Tony said sadly.

Sal looked hard at Tony. Tony sat down and explained. As he finished, he said, "So are you really thinking about being a full-time newsboy? If you are, we should do it together. We always wanted to."

"Yes," said Sal, "let's."

And with a little talk about how impossible their fathers were, it was as simple as that.

On Monday morning they met in their downstairs hall, Tony pounding down the stairs as he always did. At one time, Tony might have tried to be quieter coming down the stairs so early in the morning. Now he knew that just about everyone in the building was up at that hour, getting ready for another back-breaking day of work.

Like conspirators, Tony and Sal stole away into the pre-dawn darkness, doing what they had done so often but doing it now as partners. Senior newsboys now, they'd go to Chatham Square in the morning and then to Sal's spot on Chambers Street in the afternoon.

In the distribution room at the *Tribune*, they stood at the front of the line. Alfie and Buzz weren't there. Tony hadn't seen them in a while. He asked Sal if he knew them.

"I think so. A thin, blond kid and a short, dark-haired one. Always together."

"That's them."

"Nice, always friendly."

"Yeah, terrific," said Tony, wondering all the while

what might have happened to them and hoping they were all right. But there was no use dwelling on it. Who knew what could happen to any of them?

Tony and Sal got their papers and left for Chatham Square, where they were an immediate success. Old hands at the game, they worked the "last paper" trick and Alfie's "influencer." But never before had they made the headlines work so well for them.

No wars had broken out, but on June 1, a flood had drowned thousands and washed out railroad and telegraph lines all over Johnstown, Pennsylvania. More reports were still coming in, and trumpeting the headline "Despair Felt in Johnstown! There May Be 10,000 Dead!" put their sales over the top.

At the same time, James G. Blaine, Secretary of State, was delaying the American treaty with Samoa. Chief Red Cloud was refusing to sign a treaty granting more land to the United States Government. A Dr. Cronin had been murdered in Chicago. On 14th Street, the Church of the Immaculate Conception had been struck by lightning.

Tony and Sal alternated the top stories. Sometimes Tony shouted about Johnstown or James Blaine or Chief Red Cloud, and sometimes it was Sal. But apart from Johnstown, the stories that sold best were Dr. Cronin and the ruined church. As usual, no one could resist mayhem or disaster.

By the end of the morning, they had sold out. Elated, they stopped for sandwiches and sodas, then went on to Chambers Street.

The afternoon was slower. People were at work. They weren't around buying papers. Then with the rush hour, everything got busy again. When they finally quit just before dark, Tony and Sal had sold out a second time and had made close to 80 cents each, tips included.

For the moment, all thoughts of doing something different vanished. They started for home.

As they reached Mulberry Street, a crowd appeared. People were gaping at something, but it was hard to tell what it was.

Tony and Sal pushed closer and saw that a horse had died on the street. It lay on its side, with its legs tangled up in the traces of the wagon it had been pulling.

There was nothing unusual in this. Horses died every day all over New York City—from overwork, old age, the mid-summer heat, or the winter cold and snow. Frequently they died in harness and were left where they lay, adding to the stench of the city until the sanitation department came to cart them off.

What *was* unusual was the man with the whip.

He was cracking it at the dead animal and cracking it again, slicing its flesh and drawing blood. "Get up!" he shouted, "get up, you wretched beast! I have to make my delivery!"

Again the whip came down. "What's the matter with you?" the poor man screamed, oblivious to everyone and everything around him.

Suddenly the whip slipped from his hands. His shoulders fell. He burst into tears. A man appeared and led him away.

A shiver seemed to go through the crowd. For a moment, nobody moved. It was as if everyone who had witnessed this scene needed to reflect upon it a little. Then everyone moved at once, vanishing completely into the human flood of Mulberry Street.

Tony tried to speak. He looked at Sal. Sal touched him on the shoulder.

At home that night, Mamma was full of conversation about Signora Biondo. The poor woman had broken her arm and had to risk going to a hospital.

Vinnie just wanted to talk about the Stabile Bank. Then finally he remembered and looked at Tony. "How was your first day without me?" he asked.

Tony smiled. "Fine, we outsold you," not wanting to be mean but enjoying it a little.

"Oh," said Vinnie, "good for you."

But Tony wasn't really interested in conversation or in bragging about this first good day with Sal. The image of the whip rising and falling, rising and falling on defenseless flesh kept going through his mind. How crazy did you have to be—how driven by fear and poverty—to do something like that?

When he got into bed that night, Tony buried his head in his pillow. As he drifted off to sleep, the word *hope* swept through him once again. *Hope, hope, hope.* He hoped against hope he would never be driven so far.

The next morning, he was glad to see that the horse had been taken away.

Chapter 11

Tony and Sal never said a word about the horse. Instead, they gathered their energies and returned to Chatham Square and Chambers Street and sold newspapers. Each day they egged one another on, and each day they seemed to do better.

"Extra! Extra! Read all about it! Plan for new municipal building will ruin City Hall Park!"

"Extra! Extra! Dr. Cronin inquest still underway!"

Before long, each of them was making 90 cents a day. Then they were up to 95 cents. And now that they were spending their days out in the city, they began spending more nights out too.

They were working adults. They weren't just kids working part-time or summer vacations. They had a right to independence, to lives of their own. Each night, Tony gave his earnings to his mamma, but each night he kept something back for himself. He had a right to that now, just as the family had a right to the rest.

Those first evenings out, Tony and Sal did what they had done before. They visited the candy stores, cafés, and coffee houses. They spent hours relaxing at tables along Mulberry Street, taking in the summer nights, and imagining impossible futures for themselves, the way they had those nights on their rooftop. Only now they were rubbing elbows with adults from the neighborhood, with fancy people from uptown out for an evening of slumming, with sailors and clerks, with lawyers and happy couples.

"I'm going to own the *Tribune*, you'll see!" Tony laughed.

"I'm going to own the *Tribune* with you!" crowed Sal.

Then, one night, they were talking about a saloon they'd passed on Crosby Street. "Why don't we go there?" said Sal.

"Why don't we try Nunzio's?" said Tony. "The Wayfarers always liked it. I've been curious."

"You're looking for a fight?"

Tony shrugged, feeling cocky. "Not likely. I'm still friendly."

Sal laughed. Tony did too. They paid their check and set out. Nunzio's was over on Elizabeth, down a flight of steps. They pushed open the door and eased their way through the crush at the bar.

The place was long and narrow and decorated like a

garden. The walls were covered with rose bushes painted behind white picket fences. The tables all had roses or daisies or lilies of the valley. In the middle of the room, a stone fountain with a cupid on top sprinkled streams of water. It seemed quite strange, with all the hard-drinking men and the dense trails of smoke rising to the ceiling.

Tony and Sal found their way to a table against the wall. No one seemed to notice they were underage. The waiter didn't even look at them when he asked for their order.

"I'll have a Hell Gate, please," Tony said.

Hell Gate was a popular local beer.

"I'll have one too," Sal said.

Tony looked around. The place was full of Italian men. They were crowding the bar, packing the tables, leaning against the walls. No wonder no one had bothered them. They were with their own.

The beers came. The boys clinked glasses and drank.

"I think I see a couple of Wayfarers over there," Sal said, pointing with his head. "Not Paul though. Three or four of the others."

"Is Tommy with them?" Tony asked.

Sal glanced over again. "No, I don't think so."

Tony sighed in relief. Then he looked over and waved a couple of fingers at the group. Sullenly, the Wayfarers waved back.

Tony and Sal drank some more beer. They were pleased that they could have such a casual relationship with a local gang but still nervous that they were boys drinking in a saloon.

92

"What do you think would happen if we got caught?" Tony asked.

Sal leaned across the table and placed his hand beside his mouth. "Jail," he whispered, "no question about it."

They both laughed and took another swallow.

Then, from nowhere, came a piano roll. A figure lurched forward and scrambled onto the stage at the back of the room.

The figure was a man. He wore a black-and-white waiter's uniform and an Uncle Sam top hat. He twirled his cane, did a little tap dance, then broke into a rousing version of "In the Evening by the Moonlight." When he was through, he bowed low and waited for the applause. Tony and Sal clapped loudly, along with the others.

The fellow seemed very pleased. He grinned broadly, twirled the cane again, took a few more tap steps, and began singing

> The upper ten thousand in mansions reside
> With fronts of brownstone and with stoops high and wide
> While the lower ten thousand in poverty deep
> In cellars and garrets are huddled like sheep.
> The upper ten thousand have turkey and wine
> On turtle and ven'son and pastry they dine
> While the lower ten thousand, whose meals are so small
> They've often to go without dinner at all.

As the man finished singing, he dropped his pants. His silk underwear was decorated with red and gold dollar signs.

Everyone laughed and clapped, but Tony wasn't sure

why. If poverty was so painful, why was anyone making fun of it?

"I'm not sure I liked that," he said to Sal.

"I think it's time to go," Sal replied.

For days, they returned to their coffee shops, cafés, and candy stores. Then, walking home up Broadway late one afternoon, they passed the New Oriental.

Outside hung a large canvas. It portrayed a beautiful Turkish woman dressed in beads and flowing silk, reclining on a sofa. Beside her stood a servant, protecting her with a sunshade.

"I want to go there," Tony said.

Sal knitted his brow. "Why?"

"It looks exotic."

"Our neighborhood isn't exotic enough?"

"No."

That night they went to the New Oriental. The canvas was illuminated in the darkness, and the entrance was guarded by a large doorman wearing a purple robe and turban. They sneaked past him and found themselves beside the bar in a large, elegant room.

The walls were lit by flickering gas lamps. Colorful cut-paper ornaments decorated the ceiling. Pretty waitresses were dressed in the same flowing silk as the woman on the canvas outside. They served drinks to gentlemen wearing suits and ties. A brass band was tuning up, along with a piano.

Tony and Sal fled. Here was "the upper ten thousand." They were "the lower ten thousand." Nothing had ever made it clearer.

"But it was worth it!" Tony shouted as they headed back to the Napoli. "I'm glad we went!"

"Why?" asked Sal. "Why was it worth it?"

"Just to know it's there," said Tony.

They got bolder—that is, Tony got bolder and Sal went along. Uncertain of saloons, they discovered theaters.

There were theaters all over the Lower East Side. What had been German and Irish was fast becoming Yiddish on the Bowery and Italian in Little Italy. Sprouting up on Mulberry, Spring, and Elizabeth Streets were countless storefront theaters. They showed Shakespeare, farce, melodrama, puppet shows—all of them in Italian.

Tony knew people went. It had never occurred to him to go. Then one night, he and Sal were heading toward a candy store on Elizabeth when they ran into a crowd outside the Rienzi Teatro Italiano. The performance was about to begin. The audience was ambling inside.

"Want to go?" Tony asked.

There was only one answer. They threaded their way in, paid their 10 cents at the door, and found two seats in the last row, jammed against the back wall.

The room was a small rectangle filled with folding chairs, but the people kept crowding inside. There were men in work clothes and women in peasant shawls, husbands and wives with babies and small children, and single men in groups or alone. They'd brought pasta from home to eat, and baked potatoes and hot corn that they'd bought on the street. They shouted to one another from one row to the next.

When the curtain went up on the small stage, the lights didn't go out. They stayed dim so people could continue socializing. Tony didn't care. He was too busy watching the show.

A woman, hysterical with grief, is searching graveyards for her daughter who was kidnapped by sailors 12 years earlier in Naples. The woman is weeping and wringing her hands.

Meanwhile, the daughter has become a beautiful young woman. It's been arranged that she will marry, but one of her kidnappers has fallen in love with her. To prevent the marriage, he drugs the young woman and leaves her in a graveyard, where—incredibly—her mother finds her at last.

When the curtain came down, everyone applauded. How exhilarated Tony felt, surrounded by his fellow Italians—his *compaesani* —and taken so fully out of himself into a situation that had nothing whatsoever to do with his own life!

He glanced over at Sal. "Did you like it?"

"Did you?"

"Yes!" said Tony in a rush. "It was Italy and America all at once together!"

The wildest melodramas—the ones that made him laugh and cry the most—were Tony's favorites, but he also liked a few that seemed closer to real life. One portrayed an immigrant woman about to be hanged for killing her brutal husband. Another was about a woman so beaten down by poverty that she died, leaving her two children orphans in a storm.

Then Tony discovered the Grand Duke's on Baxter Street.

It was run by the Baxter Street Dudes, a gang led by a tough named Babyface Willie. They wrote their own "blood-and-thunder" plays, which were mostly about robbing people and killing them. They gave their performances in a tiny space, using six kerosene lamps with glass shades for the footlights and a bunch of two-legged benches for orchestra seats.

What Tony liked best was to sit in the gallery—on one of the stepladders or cardboard boxes that passed for seats up there—and scream his head off. The screaming was helped along by the fact that the Baxter Street Dudes were archrivals of the Ragpickers, and that at any second, the Ragpickers might appear. The idea of watching Harry Hickey and Babyface Willie dueling down an aisle, maybe even knocking one another off, seemed wonderful to Tony. It didn't happen, but there was always the possibility.

Going to the Grand Duke's made Tony even more adventurous. He talked Sal into going up to Tony Pastor's Opera House on 14th Street and Union Square.

It was a muggy summer night. They walked up Broadway, enjoying this special moment and trying to stay as cool as they could. No one in either of their families had even thought about going to the famous

Tony Pastor's. They were so excited and so nervous that they must have been walking faster than they thought. They arrived half an hour early.

Paying their 25 cents—a huge sum for them—they climbed to seats in the gallery. Looking out at the large stage from such a height, they could see the seats below filling with people in top hats and silk dresses, newsboy caps and overalls.

Sal took off his own cap and said, "Tony, this is some place."

Tony had to agree.

They watched a man in blackface come on with a banjo and sing "Oh, Susanna." He was followed by a magician who made scarves disappear and sawed a woman in half.

And then, on came Maggie Cline, "Irish Mag" as the announcer called her.

She had long, shiny black hair. She was wearing a low-cut black evening dress and carrying a fan. As the crowd cheered, she did a low curtsy and launched into her bawdy signature song, "When Hogan Pays the Rent." She belted the lyrics so loudly that even the folks in the last row had no trouble hearing. Then she followed with "Throw Him Down, McCloskey!" her version of a boxing match.

Tony was smitten. Although he wouldn't admit it, Sal was smitten too. All the way home, they talked of nothing else.

"What did you like best about her?" Tony asked.

"I don't know," said Sal, "her voice, I guess."

"I liked her hair," said Tony. "It was the most beautiful hair I've ever seen."

The boys walked downtown, avoiding the Bowery with its honkytonks, low-end saloons, and brothels. It seemed to be growing hotter, steamier, more like the swooning days of August than mid-July. Tony was eager to get home, eager to describe Tony Pastor's and "Irish Mag" and the evening he'd just had. He knew that Papà would scoff, but Mamma would be interested. And Vinnie, Joey, and Angelina would listen goggle-eyed.

Tony and Sal reached Mulberry Street and checked the clock at the Napoli. It was later than they'd thought, almost eleven o'clock. Maybe Tony would have to wait until morning to talk about his night. Everyone could easily be asleep.

He said good night to Sal. It wouldn't be for long. They'd be seeing each other again in just a few hours.

He climbed the stairs. Would the family have gone to the roof to cool off? He'd check the apartment and see.

He reached the fifth-floor landing and walked in. The door between the front room and the middle bedroom was closed. That was odd. But then he did a double take. Spread over the sofa, where they had never been before, were the shorts and T-shirt he always wore to bed.

Chapter 12

The closed door loomed like a terrible barrier, separating Tony from his family in the same way he'd felt separated the night he'd quarreled with his father. His clothes, exposed on the sofa, looked so pathetic and out of place. It was as if, for some unknown reason, they'd been thrown out of where they belonged.

Had he been thrown out too? No one slept in the front room. Mamma kept it clean and neat—the saints and the calendar pinned to the wall, the doilies on the cabinets. It was where they worked and ate and had company. Besides, the sofa was too small to sleep on.

The door to the middle room opened. Quickly, Mamma closed it behind her. In the dim light—her hair in a braid, her nightdress touching the floor—she looked so small.

"Tonio, you are late," she said in Italian.

"Sal and I went to Tony Pastor's, Mamma!" Tony said. "There were magic acts, a beautiful singer—"

He was getting carried away. None of it was important. "Mamma," he said, "what has happened? My clothes! The sofa!"

Mamma placed a finger over her lips. "Shh, Tonio, you will wake everyone. Papà has taken a boarder. His name is Francesco Castlamarre. He comes from our village, and he is working making streets with Papà."

"But Mamma! My clothes! I can't—"

"You will have to understand, Tonio."

She took the shorts and T-shirt off the sofa, placed them on the arm, and sat down with Tony on the soft seat. It was going to have to be this way, at least for a while, perhaps for longer. Mamma reminded Tony that everything in America was so expensive and they needed the money. They always needed more money. They were fortunate that Francesco was from Teggiano. He was such a nice young man and a good worker too. Tony was sure to like him. He would be staying in the back room with Vincenzo and Giuseppe. There was no other place to make him comfortable. Tony would have to sleep on the sofa. She was sorry—she didn't like it either—but there was no other way.

"The sofa isn't big enough, Mamma!"

"You will make it big enough, Tonio. I know you will. Everyone in the neighborhood takes in boarders. We probably should have done this sooner."

"But I am making more money now—more than five dollars last week! Isn't that enough?"

"Papà doesn't think so. He is proud of you, Tonio, and how hard you are working for the family. But he is worried about the winter, when the work goes away. Francesco is a good man. We were lucky to have him come along and not mind sharing a bed."

It was no use. Papà had made his decision.

"Why didn't you tell me before?"

"It wasn't decided until this afternoon, when Papà left work. We were going to tell you at dinner, but you rushed away to meet Salvatore."

There was nothing more to say.

"All right, Mamma, all right."

Mamma stood and kissed him. "Thank you, Tonio, I knew you would understand."

She opened the middle-room door, then went to close it behind her.

"Please, Mamma, some air."

Mamma let go of the door, and it stayed open. If nothing else, the barrier was gone.

Tony went to the dank toilet in the hall, then undressed silently in the dark front room. He was so accustomed to seeing this room filled with people. It felt strange to be there alone. Standing stiffly in the dark, the chairs and table seemed reproachful, the stove an ogre squatting in the middle of the room, telling him to leave.

Tony lay down on the sofa and tried to get comfortable, first on his side and then on his back. But the seat wasn't wide enough, and his legs were too long. He tried hanging them over the arm, leaving them at an angle, bending them as much as he could. Nothing worked. He lay there perspiring, wishing the sofa had pillows like other sofas—pillows he could remove and place beneath his head on the floor. He listened to the soft breathing of his family and of the stranger, Francesco Castlamarre, who had forced him out of his bed.

Both bedroom doors were now open, but it didn't make any difference. Although the temperature hadn't been hot enough for the family to go to the roof, the night had grown steadily muggier. The air was so heavy it hardly seemed to reach the front room at all. Tony kept closing his eyes, but he couldn't sleep.

And then he had an idea. He wasn't sure it was a very good one, but he couldn't come up with anything else.

Quickly he put on his clothes and let himself out of the apartment. Quietly he crept down the stairs. In moments, he stepped out into pre-dawn New York and began walking the familiar Mott Street route.

It might have been the darkness. It might have been the hour, but the walk seemed to take much longer than usual. Finally, Tony passed the jungle blackness of City Hall Park and there it was—the only place he knew he could go—the *Tribune* building at Nassau and Spruce. He took a deep breath and walked inside.

The distribution room was full of boys. Some were standing around talking. Most were lying on the hardboard floor trying to sleep. Some wore shorts; others

103

were barefoot. Those with caps had tucked them under their heads. Everywhere there was the smell of sweat and unwashed bodies, a smell Tony had grown so familiar with at school.

Tony looked around. There was no one he knew. He found a space on the floor and settled in, taking a lesson from those already there and putting his cap under his head. It crossed his mind that this was a level of poverty and aloneness he had hoped he would never experience. This was the sort of life Alfie and Buzz knew only too well. He convinced himself that this was a sometime event, not something he would do very often or for very long.

The heat and lack of air were as intense as ever. The floor was hard, the noise continuous, the light dim but unrelenting. And yet, there was a sense of togetherness, of safety and comfort, that made Tony feel better than he could have felt on the sofa at Mulberry Street. Tony was without his family, but he slept.

A couple of hours later, he awoke. An odd commotion was underway in the distribution room.

Tony sat up. A short man with a droopy mustache and wire-rimmed glasses was gesturing to the assistant circulation manager. In the midst of all the filth and heat, the man was wearing a well-cut brown suit, a necktie, and a shirt with a wing collar.

The manager was nodding and pointing to the boys stretched out on the floor. Quickly the man brought out what looked like a box camera and set it on a tripod. He inserted a plate into the plateholder, removed the camera's lens cover, held up a frying pan, dusted it with powder, and lit it.

There was a flash! The man clicked the shutter on the camera, replaced the lens cover, and removed the plate. Then he packed up his equipment and left.

Startled, his eyes smarting, Tony realized he had just had his picture taken. But who was this man, and why had he bothered? He asked the boy lying next to him.

"I dunno," the boy said. "I think he's a reporter for the paper."

That was interesting. No one else seemed to know more. Tony thought about asking the assistant circulation manager, but he was just too tired. He went back to sleep.

A few hours later, Tony walked back to Mulberry Street to get Sal.

Sal couldn't believe his story. "You slept in the distribution room?" he said, "and somebody took your picture?"

"Yes," said Tony, "it wasn't so bad, and the picture-taking was interesting."

He described the man, the camera, the flash.

"But what were you doing there? Why weren't you home?"

"Papà has taken a boarder, Sal. I have nowhere to sleep but the sofa."

"I see. We had a boarder once. He ate too much. Papà got rid of him."

Tony laughed. "Perhaps I will be as lucky."

By now they were back at the *Tribune* offices. They picked up their newspapers and set off for Chatham Square. Tony could have been mistaken, but the stern-faced assistant circulation manager seemed a little friendlier now that Tony had spent a night on his floor.

It wasn't a heavy news day. They had to make do with "Extra! Extra! Three men, a boy, and a horse bitten by a dog in Hoboken!" By nightfall, they'd each made almost a dollar.

All day long, Tony had worried about what it would be like when he got home. He had left the house without telling anyone. What would be worse—having to explain why or having to meet the boarder?

Tony entered the apartment. Everyone was there, gathered around the table. Papà looked at him, but it was Mamma who said, "Tonio, what happened? We were so worried!"

He apologized and explained. The tension he had anticipated all day seemed not to exist. Everyone seemed glad he was home and safe and wanted to understand. He didn't mention the photographer. It seemed unnecessary in the midst of everything else.

Of course Mamma had to overdo it a little. "You slept on the floor, Tonio? Was it clean enough? Were you comfortable?"

Tony assured her that everything was fine. Then Papà introduced him to Francesco Castlamarre. They shook hands the American way.

As Mamma had suggested, Francesco was a nice young

man. He was short and thin, with wavy black hair and a gentle smile. He spoke almost no English, but that would change. Tony didn't see him as a friend, but he couldn't find anything wrong with him either.

Tony hadn't planned to go out that night. Now he resolved not only to stay home but to help out and try to make a success of this arrangement. He dried the dishes, helped Joey and Angelina with their homework, helped make artificial flowers. And that night, he stayed on the sofa.

Fortunately, the weather was a little cooler. But even so, there was no way to make up for the size and shape of something not meant to be slept on. Tony thought of asking for a pillow from one of the beds, but he knew there were no extras.

By daybreak he was exhausted and cranky. He told no one except Sal on the way to the *Trib.*

"So what are you going to do?" Sal asked.

"You'll have to start meeting me at the distribution room."

"You're serious about this?"

"I'll tell you the nights I'm going."

"I hope you know what you're doing."

A few nights a week now, Tony began sleeping on the *Tribune* floor. He told Mamma and Papà he was going to do it, and there was a discussion. They weren't happy, but they understood. There just wasn't enough room or enough money. They were trying.

A tear came to Mamma's eye. "We want you home,

Tonio," she said, holding his arm and kissing him.

"I know, Mamma. You'll see. I'll be home most of the time. I won't stay away."

But more and more, he was going to theaters with Sal, staying out late, then going down to the *Tribune* to sleep. The next evening, he would go home only to change his clothes and get ready to go out again.

He was adjusting to the conditions at the *Trib*. The boys didn't smell as bad. Sleeping in his clothes wasn't as bad either. He also made an interesting discovery. Almost every night, that same photographer came rushing through the distribution room. He didn't take another picture of the boys, but he came through.

At first, Tony didn't give it too much thought. But then one night, he was out late with Sal and decided to sleep at the *Trib*.

He started downtown by himself. It was one of those hot spells in early August, the kind that sneak under your skin with heat and damp. Tony was almost looking forward to the *Trib's* cool floor compared to the discomforts of the dreaded sofa. He'd dropped down past Canal Street and Chinatown and was nearing the Brooklyn Bridge and City Hall Park when a well-dressed drunk, wearing a top hat and carrying a cane, came weaving by him.

Tony watched him go. Ever so softly, in his drunken way, the man was singing "I'll Take You Home Again, Kathleen." Tony wished that someone had been there to take *the man* home. This was not the safest place to be in the middle of the night—especially alone, drunk, and well-to-do.

No sooner had Tony had this thought than a bunch of toughs burst out of the park and knocked the man down. His hat flew in one direction, a shoe in another. "Help!" the man shouted. "Somebody help me!"

He tried to protect his face, but someone large flipped him over and sat on him.

"Turn out his pockets," came the voice, "get all the money!"

Stunned by the attack, Tony hadn't moved. Now he recognized the unmistakable voice of Harry Hickey.

Tony had let the Ragpickers drift to the back of his mind, but now here they were again. He couldn't let them commit this vile act and get away with it. It was one against twelve, but he had to try and stop them.

He jumped on Hickey and dragged him away. Then he turned him around and punched him in the mouth.

It was one of the most satisfying things he'd ever done, but he didn't have long to enjoy it. A half-dozen Ragpickers were on him, punching and kicking.

Then Hickey realized who had wandered in on their crime. "Hey, it's our wop, Tony! Lucky us!" he shouted.

The drunken man dashed off, salvaging his hat as he ran, and the Ragpickers turned on Tony. They pulled him down and began to beat him. Tony struggled and tried to fend them off, but suddenly there was the sound of running footsteps.

"Stop! Police!" someone shouted, and Tony heard

Hickey say, "Cool it! Let's get outta here!"

The Ragpickers scattered. Tony's head was spinning. He looked up. Wire-rimmed glasses . . . droopy mustache . . . well-cut suit . . . the photographer from the *Tribune*.

Chapter 13

"Are you all right?" the man asked.

Tony propped himself up on his arms. "I think so. A little dizzy." He smiled. "No bones broken."

The man squatted beside him. "Better rest a moment. Clear your head."

The dizziness subsided.

"I admire your courage," the man said. "The odds weren't very good."

Tony shrugged. "That gang—we have a history. It was instinct, I guess."

The man nodded. "There are many surviving on that alone these days."

Tony frowned. "You mean poor people?"

"Yes—so many in the slums."

The man held out his hand. "I'm Jacob Riis, police reporter for the *Tribune*."

Tony shook the hand. "Tony Petrosino, *Tribune* newsboy."

Riis chuckled. "So you've got pluck too. I think I've seen you in the distribution room."

"I've been sleeping there some nights. I was there the night you took the picture."

"Oh, yes, the picture."

Riis sat down on the pavement beside Tony, his hands clasped in front of his knees. He had taken the picture for an article he was writing about homeless boys in the city. "Street Arabs," he called them. They lived in squalor, but they were so independent, it was difficult to help them.

Tony thought of Alfie and Buzz. Then he got indignant. "I'm not one of them, sir. My family lives in an apartment. It's just too crowded. That's the reason I stay at the *Trib*."

Riis smiled. "I know that, Tony. Just talking with you makes that clear."

He was doing much more than an article on homeless boys. Beyond his police reporting, he was writing a whole series of articles exposing the terrible conditions in the tenements. Something had to be done, someone had to tell the facts, and this was a start. Using the new technique of flashlight photography, he was taking pictures to go along with the articles. The pictures would not lie. No one could deny them.

"But I live in a tenement, Mr. Riis," Tony said. "It's not a palace, but it's not so bad—not as bad as it was in Teggiano."

"You don't live in Mulberry Bend. You don't live in Gotham Court or Jersey Street."

Jacob Riis stood up, then helped Tony to his feet. "Listen, Tony, you impress me. I'm going on an expedition tonight. Why don't you come along? You can help carry my equipment."

Tony was stunned. He was just a kid, an immigrant kid, and a newsboy at that. Sure, he was accustomed to odd hours, but it was getting very late. The invitation made no sense . . . But was he going to say no for any of those reasons?

"Thanks, Mr. Riis," said Tony. "I'd love to come."

"Good. We'll have to stop back at the *Trib* first."

Though Riis was small, he walked quickly. In fact, he seemed to do everything quickly and was always in a hurry. They reached the *Tribune* and walked into the distribution room.

"Wait here," Riis said. "I've left the camera upstairs."

Tony scribbled a message for Sal in case he got back too late to meet him. He stood by the desk, legs and arms crossed, looking aloof and pleased with himself. When Riis got back and handed him the camera and tripod, all eyes turned toward them.

They stepped out into a night gradually growing cooler. "We're going to the Bend," Riis announced.

Tony was horrified. The Bend? *Mulberry Bend?* Sure, Riis had mentioned it moments ago, but Tony never thought they'd be going there tonight. He'd spent years avoiding Mulberry Bend. He'd promised his parents he would never go there. Now here he was, going with Jacob Riis!

"Great," Tony said.

Riis smiled. "Do you mean that?"

Embarrassed, Tony looked away. "No, but I'm game."

"Just as I thought," Riis said. "I'm glad I asked you to come."

They made their way along Park Row onto Baxter Street, then up Baxter past the Five Points and into the Bend. Immediately Riis turned off into a narrow alley between two decrepit tenements. The alley was barely wide enough to walk through, the darkness so enveloping it was almost impossible to see. Tony followed closely behind Riis. The crumbling brick walls on either side seemed ready to fall on them.

Squinting hard, Tony could make out a maze of alleyways up ahead—narrow streets that angled off in different directions. And here, now, they were in a clearing filled with trash, broken bottles, and burlap bags filled with garbage. At one end of the clearing was a ruined building made of boards. It looked as if it had been kicked in the stomach and glued to the tenement in back.

"We're in Bottle Alley," Riis said. "A lot of people have been murdered here."

Tony shivered. They climbed a flight of broken wooden steps, went inside, and knocked on a door.

It opened—to the frightened face of a woman who was filthy and dressed in rags. The two rooms of the apartment smelled of rotten food and were so filled with people there was no place for all of them to sit. There must have been at least three families—fifteen people or more—in that small space, along with a few stinking beds and a battered stove. Men, women, and children skittered away like cockroaches, not wanting to be seen but finding nowhere to hide.

"I'd like to take a picture," Riis said.

There was no attempt to resist. Quickly Riis set up the tripod and camera, flashed the light, and got his picture. The faces of the people were frozen in puzzlement and misery.

Then Riis and Tony were out and down another alley. As they hurried along, Riis asked, "How are you bearing up?"

Tony wasn't sure. Already it was worse than he'd imagined. His own difficult tenement life seemed a picnic by comparison. "I'm all right," he said.

"Good," said Riis. "I'd better tell you about the flash."

It seemed like an odd moment to choose. Tony listened.

"The powder's magnesium powder, blown through an alcohol flame. I light it in the frying pan because it seems less threatening, and it's a big improvement over the pistols we were using."

"Pistols?" Tony asked.

"When my friends and I started taking these pictures, the flashlight cartridges came in pistol lamps. We went around shooting off the pistols, and it was something to see—people diving out windows and down fire escapes in the middle of the night. Once I even set fire to a room and had to put the thing out myself."

Tony was flabbergasted. "Were you hurt?"

"It was worse when I lit the powder and blew it into my eyes. If I hadn't been wearing glasses, I'd have been blinded."

They whipped around a corner and down a few steps. They pushed open a battered door and entered a cellar. It had that sweet, pungent smell of too much beer, spilled far too often.

The room they entered was dark and grim. The gas lamps on the walls provided only the most minimal light. The floor and ceiling were scarred planks, adding more gloom to the grimness. All around, at stained wooden tables, there were men. Some wore dark suits and bowlers. Some wore open shirts and suspenders. Many were bleary-eyed and drunk or drinking or collapsed and sleeping, their heads resting on their folded arms.

"They call this a two-cent restaurant," Riis whispered. "It's really a stale beer dive. You can buy a cup of coffee and a roll for your two cents, but mostly you buy a beer and stay all night."

"Why is it stale beer?" Tony asked.

"It's the dregs—what's left over from the kegs that the saloon-keeper leaves on the street for the brewer's cart. These scavengers collect it and doctor it up with chemicals to give it a head. That's why it's so cheap. You wouldn't want to get near it."

A man began shouting in a corner. A woman, her face streaked with grime, stood up, then fell on the floor. Someone helped her stand again. She sprawled on a table and was still.

A tall man with a long nose approached Riis. "Can I help you, sir? Some coffee? A drink?"

"I'd like to take a picture," Riis said.

The man frowned. "A picture? I don't think so."

He pushed open the door, gestured with his arm.

Riis held his ground. Politely he said, "It will only take a minute. I'm Jacob Riis from the *Tribune*. I'm doing an article."

He smiled. Tony helped him set up the tripod and camera. The man held back, not ready to pick a fight. He watched as Riis lit the powder and snapped the shutter.

Then, just as quickly, Riis and Tony were gone.

"Sometimes you have to be persistent," Riis said, as they bolted through an alley he called Bandit's Roost. Menacing men leaned against the buildings or sat on stoops or poked their heads through windows. As Riis and Tony passed a corner saloon, a small boy walked in carrying a bucket. He couldn't have been more than seven. Was the beer for his father? Was it for himself and his pals, up this late and thirsty?

"That's called rushing the growler," Riis said, "taking beer home in a bucket. No child so young should be in a bar . . . but that starts me off on a whole other subject of mine: children."

Riis carried on for a while about poor children and

117

children working and how every child should have a
school to go to, a playground to play in, and a house with
a lawn, just like his own children.

When Riis was finished, Tony said, "I graduated from
eighth grade."

"Good. That's good, Tony," Riis said. He paused then
and didn't say more.

Tony wasn't sure what to say himself. Having heard
Riis speak so passionately about children and education,
he wanted to ask for his guidance. He wanted to say, "I'm
a child. I want more education. What should I do?" But
Riis didn't seem to see him that way and wasn't offering
any advice. Even if he did, what was the use? Papà still
had to approve, and he never would.

The moment passed.

Finally, Riis said, "Well, I've shown you the Bend,
which I want to see abolished. Now I'll show you the
other thorn in my side. Are you too tired?"

Tony shook his head.

They picked their way back out to Mulberry Street
and around the corner to the Elizabeth Street police
station. The sergeant on duty let them in. "Evening, Mr.
Riis," he said, smiling.

To be known by these policemen seemed to mean, at
the very least, that you'd be left alone. No one bothered
Riis and Tony as they entered the adjoining rooms, which
were divided between men and women. Each had a
beaten-up sink in one corner and a toilet in a closet in the
other. Each had a row of wooden planks on iron racks

protruding at a slight angle from the wall.

The women, glassy-eyed and misery-laden, sat together around a rusted pot-belly stove, cold now because it was summer. The men, barefoot or with dirty toes sticking through dirty socks, lay fully clothed on the hard planks. A few sat up as Riis focused the camera. Most were sleeping or paid no attention.

The stench of dirt and tragedy was so great, it was hard to stay for long. As Riis and Tony hurried away, Riis said, "I want each and every one of these police station lodging houses closed down. They do nothing but spread filth and disease."

Tony nodded. The taste of real poverty—the rock bottom of the lower ten thousand—settled under his skin as he wondered why Riis seemed angrier about the lodging houses than anything else.

Riis didn't explain. Instead he said, "I have to go back to the office now. Walk with me?"

There was no reason to go, but Tony did. As they walked back up Mulberry Street—no need to hurry now, the night's task was ended—Tony felt a certain unexpected closeness to this vigorous, friendly man with the droopy mustache. They had done something difficult together and succeeded. But as dawn began to break and they continued through Tony's neighborhood, he felt himself reclaiming his home and his family—loving them more, understanding them better.

They reached the police reporters' office at Mulberry and Houston, across from the Mulberry Street police headquarters. Even though it was so early in the morning, a few of the bearded reporters were playing cards. They looked up as Riis burst in, then went back to playing.

Riis fumbled through his mailbox, sorted out any possible leads for the next day—leads he hoped to turn into stories after a few hours of sleep. He looked up.

"I have to give a lecture tonight. Want to come again on Thursday?"

Tony would get practically no sleep tonight. Could he go out again so soon? He took a deep breath. "Sure," he said, "why not?"

"Meet me here at eleven."

Tony went home and curled up on the miserable sofa for two hours. He had never felt so glad to be in his apartment, never so relieved to be surrounded by his family and not alone.

Chapter 14

"You spent the whole night in Mulberry Bend?"

"Yes, I did."

"You weren't robbed or stabbed or anything?"

"No, I was with Jacob Riis."

It was still early the next morning. Tony had met Sal after all, and they were on their way to the *Tribune* building. Tony was filling Sal in on every detail of last night.

"I can't believe you did that," Sal said.

"Why not?"

"The Bend is a dangerous place, Tony."

"It made me realize how awful things can be for people. And flash photography is fascinating. I'm going to go again."

"You are?"

"Yes. I'll bet you could come if you wanted. I can ask Mr. Riis—"

"Never. Thanks very much."

"All right, Sal. I won't ask again."

So Tony went by himself. That Thursday night, still tired from lack of sleep, he met Riis at the Mulberry Street office. When he arrived, a tall man in uniform was also there.

"Tony, this is Sam," Riis said. "He's a public-health officer. He'll be coming with us tonight."

Tony shook Sam's hand and shouldered the camera and tripod. Once again, they set out for the Bend, but to the northern end this time, along Bayard Street. As they passed the corner of Mulberry and Bayard, Tony remembered the first time he had stood there, on that first day of school, and his encounter with the Ragpickers. It seemed so long ago, but it also seemed to have brought him to this moment.

Instinctively, he looked around. No Ragpickers.

He and the two men continued on, shadowy figures in the weak light. They walked up the steps of a tenement, Tony dragging the equipment one step at a time. They continued inside and up a battered stairway to the second floor.

The door opened. In one small room, there must have been 12 or 13 mattresses. A few were on bunks, stuffed into an alcove in the corner. The rest were wedged together on the floor. Each was occupied by a man or woman, filthy and fully clothed. With their soiled blankets pulled up around them, they were trying to sleep.

Over to one side, a worn trunk sat on top of a stove. Above it was a ragged bundle. Beaten-up boots with socks stuffed into them sat here and there. Along one wall were shelves with pots and bowls no one was going to use. A dimly burning kerosene lamp provided the only light.

Some of the men tried to hide their heads as Tony helped Riis take the picture. Another man, sitting in an alcove, grinned at the camera. No one seemed to mind the intrusion until Riis and Tony had packed everything up and Sam asked, "Who is the proprietor here?"

A weary-looking man with thin gray hair appeared, frowning.

"What are you charging these men and women?" Sam demanded.

"Five cents a space. They're here of their own free will, officer."

"I'm giving you a summons for overcrowding. Half as many lodgers are more than enough. And clean this place up. It's a pigsty!"

He handed the man a document and left. Riis and Tony followed.

The man looked after them, not reading the paper and not looking away. He looked so resigned, so weary. His eyes were wet, as if he were crying.

"Of course they won't change a thing," Riis said as the three clambered down the stairs.

"And no one will do anything about it," said Sam.

"There's no money for follow-up. Everyone's too corrupt."

"I've said it before, and I'll say it again. Tear down Mulberry Bend."

"I agree, sir. Perhaps if you keep at your work, it will make a difference."

That night, the three of them went on to a ragpicker's hovel on Jersey Street, a seven-cent lodging house on the Bowery, a Bowery saloon, and finally the Church Street police station lodging facility. As they left Church Street, Riis brightened. "How about coffee on Mulberry Street?"

The Bowery had been strangely addictive. Its combination of theaters and music halls, saloons and penny arcades, freak shows and El tracks conjured up an atmosphere of dazzle and darkness. But Mulberry Street was still Tony's greatest pleasure. *Good*, he thought. *They're taking me home.*

They went to Marietta's Cafe, a favorite haunt of Tony's and Sal's. Tony marveled at sitting there, at a table on the street, with Jacob Riis and a health officer. If his friends and family weren't all asleep, they might pass right by.

Riis pulled out a cigar. "Smoke, Tony?"

Tony shook his head. Riis offered the cigar to Sam, then lit it for himself. As their espressos arrived, Riis took a long puff, leaned back in his chair, and talked about his past and the police station lodging houses.

He had been an immigrant himself, from a little town in Denmark called Ribe. He'd sailed steerage from Glasgow and arrived at Castle Garden, just as Tony had,

124

in June of 1870. He'd had a terrible time finding work
and didn't get his job at the *Tribune* until seven years later.
At first he was a carpenter at an iron works on the
Allegheny River, then homeless and starving on these
same New York City streets. One night, in the middle of
a storm, a little dog adopted him. He brought it with him
to the Church Street Station lodging house, the very same
one they had visited tonight. The next morning, when he
complained that his treasured locket had been stolen, the
attendant threw him out and beat the dog to death on the
steps.

"I've never forgotten it, Tony." Riis said. "All the evils
of these places were summed up in that act."

Tony understood. How could he not? But he was also
understanding more: that Jacob Riis was an immigrant,
that he had spent time homeless on these familiar streets,
and that the connection between the two of them was
real.

Over the next couple of weeks, Tony went out often
on expeditions with Riis. He learned more about the
underbelly of New York—what Riis called seeing "how
the other half lives." Losing a lot of sleep, still trying to
sell his newspapers with Sal, he sometimes stumbled
because he was so tired. But he also was learning how to
use a camera—lighting the flash, setting the shutter,
removing the lens cap—all while Riis talked about
wanting to help immigrants help themselves.

One night the two of them were having their now
customary late-night coffee when Riis said, "You can do

better, Tony. You don't have to be a newsboy."

"Yes, sir, I know that," Tony said. He wondered again why Riis didn't go a step further and give him some advice. Once again, the moment unraveled.

Out of curiosity, Tony went back to the Bowery by himself the next night. He knew Sal wouldn't go, and he wanted to explore alone. He strolled into the first vaudeville theater he passed.

There was a big crowd, mostly men, showy types and a few swells who looked like pickpockets. Tony sat in the gallery trying to be inconspicuous, and the show roared past him: dogs jumping over each other; the fattest man in the world; the stage Irishman, M'hose the Bowery B'uoy, dressed in plaid pants and a stovepipe hat; a human pyramid. There was also a blackface minstrel who sang

De Camptown ladies sing dis song, Doo-dah, doo-dah,
De Camptown racetrack five miles long, Oh! Doo-dah day!
Gwine to run all night! Gwine to run all day!
I'll bet my money on de bobtail nag,
Somebody bet on de bay.

This theater wasn't as fancy as Tony Pastor's but in its scary way, it took Tony even farther from what he knew. He found himself desperate to get home. Like his first night out in Mulberry Bend, he raced back to his family. He hardly saw the streets until he reached his own, nearly flew up the stairs he'd always hated until he was at his door.

Mamma was still up, making a few extra artificial flowers. Tony threw his arms around her. "Mamma," he said, "I love you!"

Mamma giggled. "*Si*, Tonio, and I love you. Let's both get some sleep now."

Sleeping deeply despite the sofa, Tony got up in the morning refreshed. Sal was the only one he'd told about Jacob Riis. For the moment, there was no need to tell anyone else.

During the next few days, Tony just sold newspapers and tried to reconnect with his family. He played ball with Vinnie and Joey, remembering how once—so long ago, it seemed—he had enjoyed doing that. He helped his mamma with the flowers and even went out one night to play cards with Papà, Francesco, and Luigi Mazzaferri.

And then it was August 16 and the *festa* San Rocco. Of course the whole family had to go. Papà, Francesco, and Tony took the day off, and they all went together.

At eleven o'clock, they clattered down the stairs and waited in front of the building. Around them, suspended from the tenements, were tapestries and Italian flags, three-colored lanterns and strings of lightbulbs. It was like being back in Naples, and everyone in the crowd seemed happy. The women were wearing colorful dresses, the men dark suits and military society uniforms. Tony clutched Angelina's hand, the hand he remembered holding that first day on Mulberry Street. It was smaller then.

Tony knew the story of San Rocco. Suffering from plague and hunger, he'd been befriended by a dog that brought him bread from its master's table. Rocco was said to have the power to cure illnesses, and Tony wished in his heart that his family would never need such a miracle. He also reached to find a connection—healing, the need to make things better—between Rocco's dog and Jacob Riis's dog.

The procession began over on Mott Street, but moments later the trumpets sounded and flags and banners appeared. A squad of policemen came first, followed by a band, and a banner featuring San Rocco and his dog. The banner was flanked on either side by an Italian flag and an American flag. Then came the members of the Societá San Rocco, looking proud in their blue dresses with gold buttons and stripes. Behind them was San Rocco's shrine, with various wax body parts attached. The body parts symbolized the cures that had been requested: a healed leg for Mrs. Florio, restored hearing for Mr. Genovese.

There were more bands, as well as the congregations from different churches. In the midst of all the music, the firecrackers sounding up and down the street, and the cheers of the crowd, Tony put his arm around his brother Vinnie. Vinnie looked up and grinned.

But later that evening, Tony got restless. He ran downstairs and coaxed Sal into going out with him. Filled with the joy of the festival and things Italian, he wanted to go to the theater. "I want to see something different but really Italian," he said.

"We haven't been to a marionette show."

"Good. Let's go."

They remembered passing one on Spring Street, just a few blocks away, so that was where they went. Tony was hurrying Sal now the way Riis always hurried him. They hurried through the streamers, the dead firecrackers, and the paper lanterns of the festival. At one point, Sal looked down at him, a little annoyed at being rushed. Tony paid no attention; he just hurried on.

A schedule was posted on the window of the tiny storefront theater. The company was performing two play cycles on alternative nights: *The Wars of the Paladins* and Ariosto's sixteenth-century *Orlando Furioso*. Each play would take years to complete, but no one in the crowd seemed to mind. They laughed and joked as they went inside.

Tony and Sal paid their 10 cents for that evening's offering, which turned out to be *The Wars of the Paladins*. Because the tiny theater was so crowded, they couldn't sit together. Since Sal was the taller one, he would sit behind Tony on the aisle. They settled into their folding chairs.

The stage was small and only about six feet high. The curtain went up, and on came the puppets. They were three or four feet tall, with carved features and elaborate costumes that ranged from silk and velvet to full suits of armor. If Tony ducked his head, he could see the men standing on a concealed platform behind the stage, controlling the puppets' movements with long rods.

He was enthralled. With puppets, fancy costumes, and dramatic music as extras, the medieval wars of the

Paladins seemed a lot like the back-street wars staged by the Baxter Street Dudes.

After a while, though, Tony was no longer watching the stage. He was watching the doorway beside it that led to the back of the theater. Over the doorway hung a black velvet curtain. And in front of the curtain stood the prettiest girl Tony had ever seen.

Chapter 15

She was medium height, about as tall as Tony. She had long black hair, dark eyes, and a heart-shaped face. With the lights dimmed and the action onstage unfolding, it was hard to tell more. But the way she stood in front of that black curtain, with her weight on one leg and her hand on her hip, was tantalizing.

Intermission arrived. The lights came up and she was gone. What was her role in this drama? What did she do behind the scenes?

Tony went outside with Sal. He was grateful that his friend hadn't seen him staring at the girl. He wouldn't have to explain.

Tony wondered why he felt this way. Most of the time, he didn't mind telling Sal anything. They were friends. They shared their feelings. But this was too special, too private, too hard to define. If he talked about it, he might jinx it.

"What do you think of the show?" he asked instead.

Sal shook his head. "I don't get it. I don't like it. I think I'm going home."

"You are?" Tony asked.

"Yes. You want to stay?"

Want to stay? thought Tony. *Would I be anywhere else?* "Yes, I think so."

"Then I'll see you tomorrow morning."

Tony watched Sal disappear down Spring Street. Then he returned to the little theater and waited for the second act.

Around halfway through, the velvet curtain parted and she was there. But once again, as the performance ended, she disappeared.

Tony stayed in his seat as long as he could after the applause ended and the audience left. Then he stood up, lingering. He wondered what he could do before someone came along and threw him out. There was only one choice. He took a breath, gathered his courage, and walked through the black curtain.

Nothing happened. He found himself backstage, in the area just behind the platform where the puppeteers stood holding their rods. Several of them were packing up their gear and talking to one another. A boy, obviously an assistant, carried two puppets toward the stage door.

Suddenly she was there, speaking firmly to another puppeteer, asking him to take his puppets to the back of the theater.

Tony stood still.

She noticed him. She came over. "Can I help you?" she asked with a smile so broad that Tony was lost for words.

She came closer. "Do you want something here?"

You, Tony wanted to answer. *Just you. Nothing but you.* He tried to speak. "I saw you from my seat. I wanted to meet you."

He had never done something like this before. He had no idea what might happen now.

"I'm sorry," she said, "I think you'll have to leave."

That wasn't what he had hoped for. "I can't do that," he said. "Please have coffee with me."

"Have coffee with you? I don't even know you."

She walked to the stage door and opened it.

"Please. My name is Tony Petrosino. I know you will like me."

She was still holding the door open, but the smile was there again. "You're very persistent, aren't you?"

"Mr. Riis says sometimes you have to be."

"Who?"

"I'll explain over coffee."

She was weakening. She took her hand off the knob. She closed the door and pulled him aside.

"I can't come. My papà won't let me."

He was looking at her hair—that long, shiny black hair that reminded him of Maggie Cline, the singer at Tony Pastor's. "But I have to see you. When can I see you again?"

Her eyes danced. The edges of her mouth turned up in a little grin. "After the performance tomorrow night. I'll try to get away. Tell me where to meet you."

Tony had to think fast. He'd never asked a girl to meet him anywhere. "There's a candy store at the corner of Broome and Mulberry. The Napoli."

"All right. I'll be there. Ten o'clock."

"I'm so glad. Your name?"

"Maria Cavellino."

She was gone again, somewhere in the darkness of the theater. Tony let himself out the stage door and started for home, clutching a fistful of doubts and possibilities.

He had met her. She was wonderful—the most wonderful, beautiful person he had ever met. She seemed to like him. She had said she would come tomorrow night, but what if she didn't show up? And why had he chosen the Napoli, the candy store closest to his house? What if Sal came in? What if Papà or Francesco saw them? He'd be nervous and worried the whole time. Even so, he was going to see her again! That had to be enough, didn't it? All the way home, and then all night long on the sofa, he agonized as he tried to fall asleep.

Selling his newspapers with Sal the next day, Tony was too distracted to talk very much. "You've been very quiet," Sal said as they walked toward Mulberry Street.

"Just tired," Tony explained. "I'll get to bed early tonight."

It wasn't a lie exactly—maybe only a half-truth—but Tony had never avoided an issue like this before. Certainly not with Sal. On the brighter side, he realized he had just given himself the evening free . . . But what if Sal showed up at the Napoli? It would make things even worse.

There was nothing Tony could do. Just before ten o'clock, he excused himself from the kitchen table, said he was going out, and crossed the street to the candy store. He said *buona sera* to Mr. Benevento—who would also know that Tony had been there with a girl! Then he sat down at a table facing away from the window. It was another warm night. He ordered a cherry soda.

The tables were crowded. No one he knew was there.

Ten o'clock. No one came. Tony waited. Ten-fifteen. Ten-thirty. He was so embarrassed. First he had to pretend he was waiting for someone who was just a little late. Then he had to admit he'd probably been stood up.

At ten forty-five, Tony rose, paid for his soda, and left. He hoped no one had bothered to notice him.

So the worst had happened. She hadn't come. His heart was black. He'd never see her again. . . . But could something have interfered? Could there be a reason? He had to know.

He went straight to Spring Street. The theater was closed and dark, not at all welcoming. He knew he should just go home and forget the whole thing, but he couldn't.

He stood there, minute after minute, and a miracle happened. The door opened and out stepped Maria Cavellino.

Tony was so surprised that all he could do was say the wrong thing. "How did you know I was here?" he asked.

"I didn't. I was just leaving. I'm sorry I couldn't meet you."

He wanted to take her in his arms. Instead he said, "What happened?"

"It was Papà. He must have suspected something. He kept me in the office, going over ticket receipts."

She looked over her shoulder. "He'll be coming in a minute. You can't be here talking to me."

Tony was going to lose her again. "Can I see you tomorrow night?"

There was that smile again—that wonderful, disarming smile. "You are persistent, aren't you?"

"Yes."

Maria looked over her shoulder again. "All right. Ten o'clock. Barbera's. It's a coffee house on Prince Street. Now go."

Tony went, vanishing around the corner into Mulberry Street before Papà Cavellino's footsteps could be heard in the hall. He would meet her at Barbera's, he was sure of it. He wasn't going to worry at all that night or the following day.

He didn't worry, and he was there, right at ten o'clock. Around two corners from the theater, Barbera's was a pleasant little place with round tables and wrought-iron chairs. He'd said he was going out, told Sal he was busy. Now where was she?

At ten-fifteen she swept in, hair flying. Her dark eyes searched the room. "Oh, there you are," she said, flopping into the chair across from him. "I'm sorry I'm late.

Everything went wrong tonight. At least I made it, though."

She smiled. She didn't have to do more.

"I'm glad you're here," Tony said.

They ordered coffee, and Maria talked a little about herself. As Tony knew by now, her father was the owner of the theater. Even though she was only 15, she was his special assistant. That meant she had to be there with him every night and look after absolutely everything, from the puppets and the puppeteers to the costumes and the theater itself. The only things her father seemed to look after were the books. But the theater didn't make much money, so her Mamma had to take in sewing. And on top of everything else, she, Maria, the only child, had to work six days a week as a sales girl at the A.T. Stewart department store on Broadway!

"That's some store," Tony said.

"Yes, but not when you have to be there every day, standing on your feet and trying to be nice to people who treat you badly."

Maria and Tony were both immigrants. She was from Calabria and had been in America for five years. They had both finished eighth grade, although Maria's' father had felt that school was useless for girls and tried to keep her from going.

"My papà felt the same way about boys going to school," Tony said. "I wanted to continue after eighth grade, but he wouldn't let me."

"These papàs," Maria said, "they're very strict. All they

care about are family and traditions from the Old Country."

"I know, but family is important. I just wish Papà understood more about America."

"My papà," Maria said, "he wants to tell me what to do about everything. Where I can go. Who I can go with. He wants me to make the best marriage, no matter what I think about it. You would not be good enough for him. He would never let me see you if he knew I wanted to."

Her words hung in the air. Tony knew that his father would never let him see Maria because he hadn't given his approval first. Tony also knew that he would risk his father's anger all over again to be able to see her. Perhaps when Papà finally learned about Maria, he could be made to understand. Tony asked the question.

"Will you see me again?"

Maria's mouth opened. She put her hands in her lap and looked down. Then she looked up at Tony and smiled. "Of course I'll see you. I don't know how, but I will."

Tony was so relieved. Clearing his throat, he said, "I have an idea. We don't work far from each other. Why don't we walk over the Brooklyn Bridge tomorrow at lunchtime?"

It was arranged. Papàs would be nowhere in evidence. But now they had to go home.

As they were getting up, Maria asked, "Who was that man you mentioned—Mr. Riis?"

Tony laughed. "You remembered."

He explained, not going into all the details but telling her some of the story.

Maria's reaction was a lot like Sal's. "You were in Mulberry Bend at two in the morning?"

Tony explained some more, describing the plight of the homeless and what Riis wanted. He promised he would never ever take Maria to such places himself. As he continued, he realized he'd been out of touch with Riis for more than a week now. He wanted to be back in touch but felt awkward about using the phone number he'd been given. He found himself becoming absorbed in Maria instead.

Outside in the street, Tony knew he couldn't walk Maria home. "Sleep well," he said. "See you tomorrow."

She touched his hand. "Yes, tomorrow."

He was thrilled, absolutely thrilled. But if he was going to have lunch with Maria, he couldn't have lunch with Sal. He would have to tell Sal about her.

He waited until late in the morning, just after Sal had made a four-cent tip. When he told him, Sal almost dropped the nickel.

"You mean after I left you that night —?" he began.

Tony nodded.

Sal blushed. "I don't believe it. Tony, you are something else!"

Tony smiled. "It's all true."

Sal put his arm around him. "Good luck, my friend. Your papà will kill you, but I'll see you after lunch."

Sal's remark echoed in Tony's head. He walked quickly over to the bridge. Perhaps he could keep Papà from

knowing until Maria's father had approved of him. Then
Papà would have to go along. But Maria's father would
never approve. It was all completely hopeless.

It didn't matter now. He wanted to see her. He had to
see her. Would she be late again? Would she even come?
Was their meeting last night nothing but a foolish dream?

He approached the bridge, its tall towers soaring above
him. And there she was, waiting at the entrance, wearing
a long blue dress. Its round collar framed her perfect
neck. Her dark hair fell around her shoulders. She was
beautiful, so beautiful.

Tony walked up to her, and she smiled. "I beat you,"
she said. "I'll bet you didn't think I would."

Tony shook his head. "I didn't, but you did."

He took her arm, impressed with his boldness, and
paid the penny apiece it cost to cross. Then, a bit
hesitantly, they started on the pedestrian walk to the
Brooklyn side.

It was so far down to the East River below, it was
dizzying to look. But Tony discovered that if he looked
out or up, not down, it wasn't so bad. In fact, it was
breathtaking, like nothing else he had ever seen. How
could he never have done this before?

They walked to the center of the bridge and stopped,
looking at the magnificent double arches at each end, the
thick cables between them, and the rising skyline of
Manhattan to the left. The ferry boats, with their tall
black smokestacks, made their way back and forth across
the river.

There was a breeze in their hair despite the hot day,

and they felt comfortable. How soothing it was just being together with no one else to bother them.

A carriage came by. Tony protected Maria from the rumbling wheels.

"Isn't this incredible?" he said.

She nodded.

He took her hand. They walked the rest of the way across, indulging themselves in silence. They walked faster now, knowing there would be only a little time to grab a sandwich from a corner stand.

As they finished eating, Tony said, "Maria, I—"

She placed a finger over his lips. "I know, Tony, I know."

But what did she know? Did she know how much he cared about her? Did she know how much he feared their fathers? Did she care about him too? She took her finger away.

"Sunday afternoon," he said, "I could get away then. Let's walk to Central Park."

It had to be carefully planned. There was a show at the theater Sunday night, so they couldn't get back late. They would meet at one at the corner of Prince and Mulberry, far enough away from anyone they didn't want to see them. No one would be told except Sal.

The rest of the week couldn't go by fast enough for Tony. He arrived at Prince and Mulberry 10 minutes early.

Maria, who was five minutes late, came running. "I'm sorry," she said. "Papà wouldn't believe I was going out with my girlfriends."

"How did you convince him?" Tony asked, realizing at once that it wasn't important.

Maria was about to say something.

"It doesn't matter," Tony said, hoping she wouldn't think he was being rude. "I'm just happy you're here," he added, hoping that would explain. "Well, let's get started."

He wanted to put his arm around her but took her hand instead because he had done that before. She didn't protest. She smiled that radiant smile, and they walked over to Broadway on this cool, crisp, late-August day.

Broadway. The first avenue Tony had ever been on in America. The avenue he and Sal had walked to see Irish Maggie Cline. Watching at each corner for passing carriages and horse cars and standing between Maria and the street to keep her from flying garbage and manure, Tony led the way uptown as far as Waverly Place. "I'm taking you to Washington Square—*George* Washington Square—Park." he said.

"Why?" she asked.

"You'll see."

He led her to the statue of Garibaldi, only recently put up. There the great soldier stood, one knee thrust forward, hand on his sword.

"I haven't seen it before," Tony said. "I only just heard about it. I wanted to see it with you."

Maria squeezed his hand. "Do you think Garibaldi was a very nice man?"

Tony shrugged. "I don't know. He's a hero."

Chapter 16

Although it was small and not very interesting, something about Washington Square Park impressed Tony. Maybe it had something to do with the combination of George Washington and Garibaldi—the great American and the great Italian—somehow joined together here. Tony liked the idea of the combination. It was the combination he felt inside himself.

He tried to explain this to Maria. She seemed to understand, but for the time being she was much more interested in the buildings on Fifth Avenue. They passed a few stately mansions, and then at 23rd Street, there was the Fifth Avenue Hotel. It was elegant and aglow in white marble, with columns out front.

"Oh, my goodness," Maria said.

They stood and looked at it for a while. They thought about going in to see the lobby, but they were too afraid.

"I'd like to stay in a place like that with you someday," Tony said, though he didn't mean it the way it might have sounded.

Maria blushed. "What a nice thing to say."

Still holding hands, they peered into the window of Delmonico's Restaurant, admiring the crisp white tablecloths and the polished silver. They continued uptown, passing brownstone houses, majestic churches, and more huge mansions. The mansions looked like palaces in a fairyland.

Then they were in Central Park, and it really was a fairyland. Not since Teggiano had Tony seen such a wide expanse of green. But this was all green grass, and it was carefully mowed and looked after. There were gentle paths running over hills and under bridges. There were trees and a pretty lake with rowboats and men in striped shirtsleeves, rowing ladies with colorful parasols. Men and women strolled the paths. Some of them were arm-in-arm, others were wheeling baby carriages.

On a bridge overlooking the lake, Tony put his arm around Maria. As they walked on, imagining themselves like the other couples, Tony said, "We're doing now what I've always wanted to do with my family. There has never been time."

"Not for me either," Maria said. "Papà hardly ever leaves Spring Street."

"Can we do more?" Tony asked.

"I hope so."

The mention of her father and the "hope so" cast a

momentary shadow on the bright afternoon. But soon they were cheerful again and walking arm in arm.

It grew late. There was no time to walk home. They would have to take a horse car.

Tony complained about having to spend the 10 cents for two fares. Maria consoled him and poked fun at him too. The two of them held each other close all the way downtown.

They decided to meet Tuesday after work. They could steal a few hours before Maria had to be at the theater.

For Tony, the time crawled by. Then there they were, touching hands in City Hall Park, and everything was all right again.

"Let's go look at the Statue of Liberty," Maria said.

They hurried downtown while it was still light. They leaned against the railing in Battery Park and looked out at the Lady of the Harbor.

"She's the first thing I saw when I came here," Tony said, remembering.

"Me too," said Maria.

"She's beautiful."

"Beautiful," Maria murmured, putting her head on Tony's shoulder. Then, "Tony, I'm worried."

"Why?" he asked, but he knew before she said a word.

"What if Papà finds out?"

"He won't. And if he does, we'll talk to him. We'll make him understand."

He turned her to him and kissed her. Then they started back uptown. They talked about maybe going to

Coney Island over the weekend and what fun they would have if she could get away.

On Mott Street, they ducked into a doorway for one last kiss before parting. It was a long kiss and lovely. Suddenly—he didn't know why—Tony opened his eyes. Standing in the doorway, his mouth a perfect *O*, was Luigi Mazzaferri! Where had he come from? What was he doing there? Luigi scuttled away.

"Oh, no," Tony said, holding Maria tight.

"What's the matter?"

Tony explained.

Maria looked scared. "What will happen now?"

"I don't know. Nothing I hope."

But Tony knew better. The hated, fawning Luigi— Luigi, the spineless creep—would go straight to Tony's papà. He would gain favor and a pat on the head, all at Tony's expense.

Papà would be home from work by now. Papà would know about Maria before Tony got home.

Walking Maria as far as the corner of Mott and Prince, Tony held her extra tight. She recognized his fear and held him too.

At the corner, trying to pretend nothing had happened, they agreed to meet for lunch on Thursday. He kissed her quickly, and she was gone. Gone.

Tony watched her as she walked away. Then, preparing for the inevitable clash, he took a walk around the neighborhood.

How odd that Maria had been so worried that *her*

father would be the one to find out. And yet, surely it did not matter. Once Tony had explained—once his papà knew how wonderful Maria was and how perfect they were for each other—he would have to be happy for them.

Tony smiled wistfully, knowing how unlikely that was to be. He walked around until it got dark. Then, his heart pounding, he started for home.

There was the familiar, crowded street and then the familiar door. Tony opened it and started up the stairs, remembering the last time they had seemed like a stairway to the unknown. But last time, everything had been worked out. He had become a newsboy, not the worst thing that could happen. He had regained his papà's love. Somehow, this time, maybe it would all work out again.

As he reached the fifth floor landing, he wasn't so sure. He waited—and opened the door.

Papà was standing. Vinnie was in front of him, eyes downcast. Papà was wagging his finger. "You must pay for the window out of your own money, Vincenzo. You broke it with the baseball. What else can you do?"

"But Papà, it wasn't my fault," said Vinnie. "Gino was on first base, and—"

They both realized that Tony had come in. Vinnie looked back over his shoulder.

Papà exploded. "You!" The shout was so loud it must have been heard all over the neighborhood. "My eldest son, my smart one, you did this to your papà!"

Mamma came running out of the bedroom and threw

herself around Papà's neck. "Pietro, no, please!"

He thrust her away, as if she were nothing. "You, Tonio, are seeing a girl I have not chosen! You are spending this family's money on her!"

Tony wanted to stop his father and tell him that he loved him. He wanted to say that he had done nothing wrong, that this was America and things were different here. But he could not.

"Leave this house!" Pietro bellowed. "Leave this house and do not come back!"

The shout was so loud, so all-enveloping, it was as if Tony had been blown out the door. He found himself on the landing. He stumbled down the stairs as if he were dreaming.

He crossed the street and sat down at a table in front of Marietta's. It was the same table where he had sat so often with Sal or Jacob Riis. He couldn't bear to see either one of them now. He couldn't bear to see Maria. What could he possibly say?

He sat at an angle, facing in such a way that anyone coming from his house would be sure to see him and could invite him in if they wished. But no one appeared, and no one invited him anywhere.

He wasn't hungry. He couldn't possibly eat. He ordered an espresso and sat there with it, not drinking.

So now he was truly alone. During these last weeks, he had understood all over again the closeness of his family ties. But now he had fallen in love with Maria and lost it all. Why was falling in love such a crime?

This time, there was no hope. He *had* been thrown out of his family. He was a homeless person, like the wretches he had seen with Jacob Riis. He would become a "street Arab," condemned to living in doorways and police station lodging houses. He'd grow dirtier and more deranged, and colder and colder in the winter. He thought of that poor man beating his dead horse, of the low end of the lower ten thousand. Now when he went to sleep on the *Tribune* floor, it wouldn't be for convenience. It would be because he had nowhere else to go.

It got late. If he was going to sell newspapers tomorrow, he would have to get some sleep. He paid for his coffee and stood up. There was, of course, no choice. He headed for the *New York Tribune*.

Down the familiar dark streets, down into the bowels of lower Manhattan, so quiet and deserted at this hour. Here was City Hall Park, where he'd touched Maria's hands and where, not so long ago, he'd played the hero and Jacob Riis had rescued him. He stopped and looked around, remembering.

"Hey, looky here!" came the voice. "We've missed you, Tony. Ain't no one around to save you now!"

Hickey, of course, Hickey. Why had he been so dumb, standing in the darkness, almost as if he were waiting? Was this the fate he had dodged for so long—the fate that had now caught up with him? He realized that it didn't matter. He didn't care.

The Ragpickers were on him in a moment, punching, kicking, elbowing him to the ground. Weakly he put up his fists to defend himself, but it was no use. He tried to curl into a ball but failed as Hickey pushed a boot into his face.

The blows rained down. The last thing Tony heard before he passed out was Hickey's wild cackle, "That's all for you, wop!"

Chapter 17

He had no idea how long he had lain there. Consciousness returned slowly, and it seemed to arrive with the sun. His face hurt pretty badly. He opened his eyes.

A young-looking man was watching over him. He had bright blue eyes and a shock of brown hair that fell over his forehead. Crouching beside Tony, he brushed the hair away with his hand.

"Are you badly hurt?" he asked.

Tony shook his head. "I don't think so. I don't know."

"Can you stand?"

Tony tried. His legs were wobbly and sore, but he didn't fall.

"Good," said the man. "You were out very cold."

Tony tried to smile. "The Ragpickers have a way of

151

doing that." He felt in his pockets. "I had a couple dollars. They took them too."

"I know the gang," said the man. "Real troublemakers. Can I take you somewhere?"

Tony lowered his eyes. "I've got nowhere to go."

"I see. Well, let me take you somewhere anyway. You'll want to clean up, recover, get your bearings."

"Who are you? Why do you want to help a lousy newsboy?"

"Nick Dale. I work for the Children's Aid Society."

Tony bristled. "You're not going to send me out West!"

Nick laughed. "No, no, don't worry. The Society does a lot more than send orphans to farms—"

"I'm not an orphan!" Tony snapped.

"I didn't say you were. Look, just let me take you to the Duane Street Lodging House. You're a newsboy. You'll find a lot of newsboys there."

No more questions. Straight to the point. Tony liked that. He remembered the Duane Street Lodging House. Alfie and Buzz had mentioned it a lifetime ago.

"All right," he said, "I'll go."

It wasn't far, only a few blocks, at the corner of Duane and Chambers. They walked slowly, Nick holding Tony's arm. Tony was reminded of taking Maria's arm. He tried not to think about that.

Arriving at the lodging house, he saw a sign over the door: "Boys who swear and chew tobacco cannot sleep here." Tony remembered Alfie and Buzz saying the place had a lot of rules. He was too tired to mind.

Nick took charge of the paperwork, and Tony was checked in. Nick smiled. "I'll stop back tomorrow. Make sure you're all right."

"Thank you," Tony said. He couldn't think of any more words.

He was shown to the washroom. It was a long, narrow room with wood paneling and a sink like a trough along one wall. He washed his face and hands, letting the water clean the cuts in his cheek and soothe the swelling over his eye. Then he went upstairs to the dormitory.

It was large and painted white, with row after row of bunk beds made up with crisp white sheets and pillowcases. The foul triple bunk beds on the White Star Line flickered across his mind. Never had he seen sheets and pillowcases as clean as these.

The room was empty. All the boys were out working. Tony chose a lower bunk from among the wealth of possibilities. He took off his clothes, crawled between the sheets, and slept.

When he awoke, it was late in the day. The room was still, but he could hear a crowd of boys gathering downstairs in the dining room. His face still hurt, but he realized he was hungry. He got up, put on his clothes, and followed the noise. All the while, he wondered how he could be going to dinner in a lodging house. Going to dinner without his family.

He got in line, got his plate of pork and beans, and sat down at a table. Other boys were staring—he was the new one, the stranger—but he paid no attention. He ate his food and kept his eyes on his plate.

Suddenly there was a shout. "Hey, it's our pal Tony! What are *you* doin' on Duane Street?"

Tony looked up. It was Alfie. Buzz was right behind him. They rushed over and shook hands as Tony avoided their question.

"It's been a long time," Alfie said.

"Months," said Buzz.

"Yes," said Tony. His thoughts tried to find their way back to the last time he'd seen Alfie and Buzz. "An awful lot has happened."

Having made that remark, Tony was sorry. It gave Alfie the opening to ask his question again. Fortunately he didn't. He just plunged ahead with his own story.

"Yeah," he said, "we gave up bein' newsboys for a while, decided we'd be busboys in a restaurant. It wasn't for us—too confinin'—so we're back on the street again, like always."

Tony smiled but had no reply. He was glad Alfie and Buzz were so cheerful about their failures. It made everything seem a little less gloomy. But their appearance out of nowhere only made this moment more unreal.

As if noticing Tony's face for the first time, Alfie said, "Hey, Tony, somebody beat you up pretty bad."

Tony blinked. He knew he had to say what had happened. So he did, telling more than he would have wished, all of it flowing out like liquid from a bottle. Maria. His father. The Ragpickers. Somehow he managed to avoid mentioning his exploits with Jacob Riis. They didn't seem like something Buzz and Alfie would understand.

154

When Tony finished, Alfie laughed. "So now you're stuck with us."

Tony frowned. He shouldn't have told his story. He hadn't meant it to sound like that.

"Welcome to the group," Buzz said.

It was strange. By falling to the bottom and admitting it, he'd insulted his friends, who were already there.

"I guess we'd better be goin'," Alfie said.

"Yeah, see ya 'round," Buzz said.

Tony nodded, wondering if he'd ever see them again.

They were gone, and he was alone. Once he no longer had them in front of him, he wondered if he had imagined their visit. It was good to be alone, though. He went back to the dormitory and slept again.

In the morning, Nick Dale was sitting at the foot of Tony's bed. The shock of brown hair was still falling over his eyes.

"Hello. How are you feeling?"

His words were simple and obvious, but there was something so sincere about them, Tony felt cheered. He smiled. "Better."

"How are the wounds?"

The pain was less. There was a tightness in his cheek. He touched the swelling over his eye. "Also better."

"Good. I think you'll want to rest for the next couple of days. Then we'll see."

Having had to make all his own decisions until now—some of them not so wise—Tony was grateful to have someone making decisions for him. Nick accompanied him to breakfast—bread and a cup of good strong coffee. He explained the way the Duane Street Lodging House worked.

Tony's bed would cost six cents a night, each meal another six cents. The house would lend him enough money to get back on his feet as a newsboy or anything he might choose. An account would be kept of these expenses, and when he had made enough money, he would pay them back. If he wished, he could keep his savings in a locked box that would be opened once a month.

Fair, fair, all fair. It crossed Tony's mind that he would have money for the locked box since he'd no longer be giving money to his family. He pushed the thought away and turned to look at Nick.

"Where will you be?" he asked.

"I'll be around," Nick said.

And he was. Over the next several days, he was at the foot of Tony's bed each morning. They had breakfast together, and sometimes he dropped by at dinner. Tony learned that one of Nick's ancestors, Sir Thomas Dale, had been an early governor of Jamestown, Virginia, the first English colony in what would become America. Sir Thomas had built stockades to imprison criminals, but he'd also encouraged the tobacco trade and friendship with the Indians.

"I guess I see the world the way Sir Thomas did," Nick said, twirling the spoon in his coffee cup. "Hard work, cooperation, punishment when necessary."

Tony took it all in. No one had ever spoken to him with such thoughtful intelligence before. Not even Jacob Riis. He was glad to listen, even when he didn't fully understand. He told Nick about his interest in education.

"You know, the Society has a number of industrial schools," Nick said at one point.

Tony had heard about those schools. "I'm not sure a trade is what I want," he said.

But mostly during those days, Tony was alone, trying to pull himself together and heal. He had no interest in the other boys. They seemed to understand and gave him a wide berth.

On the second afternoon, he discovered the gymnasium on the top floor. For some reason, it had a trapeze swing. Since no one was there during the day, Tony was able to rock back and forth, uninterrupted, for as long as he liked. He thought about Maria and how he'd missed his lunch appointment with her. He thought about Sal and missing their daily round. He didn't know if he could face Maria. He knew he had to face Sal.

By Saturday he was ready.

"Good, Tony," Nick said. "I'm proud of you."

They shook hands. Tony grinned. No one had been proud of him for some time. The words made him feel stronger.

It was too late to meet Sal at the *Tribune* building, so Tony went straight over to Chatham Square. As he'd expected, Sal was already underway, hawking his newspapers in a loud, confident voice. "Cronin murder suspects in court! Read all about it!"

When Sal saw Tony crossing the street, he looked as if he'd seen a ghost. "Tony, where have you been?" he asked. "What happened to your cheek?"

"I'll tell you," said Tony, "but you won't believe it."

He told the whole story, including Nick and the lodging house and even the trapeze swing.

"Of course I knew about your family," Sal said at the end. "The whole block knows. But I was worried about you."

Tony wanted to hear what the block was saying, but of course he already knew without having to ask.

"Are you ready to come back to work?" Sal asked.

Tony was overjoyed. Here was someone with faith in him, someone who trusted him.

"Yes," he said, "I am."

"Then go get yourself some papers."

So they were back in business. Only now, when work was done for the day, Tony went back to the lodging house instead of Mulberry Street. Each evening when he would say goodbye to Sal, he'd feel a twinge in his heart. Would he ever get his family back? Would he ever get Maria back?

On that first Sunday after Tony rejoined Sal, Nick showed up at breakfast for moral support. When Tony had gone over his hurt again, Nick said, "Look, you're doing well. One step at a time. But if you ever need me, call."

So this was the last visit. When Nick had gone, Tony felt a loss. But he told himself that it was only because he had come to welcome that smiling face, that loose shock of hair, each morning. Of course Nick had to go back to his own life. The only choice for Tony was to go on with his, taking one step at a time.

For the next month, he did exactly that. He sold his papers with Sal, paid off his debt at the lodging house, and saved money in the locked box. Often he wanted to go back and talk with his father, but he was sure he'd be unwelcome and did not. He wanted to see Maria but was too embarrassed, too uncertain of what to say. He didn't even go out with Sal the way he used to. He just didn't have the energy.

Then one night, he got restless. He'd been thinking about losing contact with Jacob Riis. At first, Maria had distracted him. Then the terrible humiliation of becoming a homeless person kept him away. He remembered the saloon they'd been to on the Bowery. He decided to go again for old time's sake.

The saloon was mostly Irish and sandwiched between a theater and a peep show, but Tony walked right in. He stood at the bar and ordered a Hell Gate.

He took a long swig. It was good, and he felt just fine. He looked down the bar and noticed a black man wearing a bowler hat.

Tony moved closer. The man was less dignified than he'd first appeared. His pants were stained and his black suit jacket was torn around the lapel. But he looked friendly. Feeling sure of himself, Tony began a conversation.

The man's name was Jess Parker. His parents were former slaves. They'd come north after the Civil War and become domestic servants on Fifth Avenue. Jess was the coachman for the family his parents had served his whole life. He'd always lived on Thompson Street, but now the neighborhood was being taken over by Italians.

"That's amazing," Tony said. "We're almost neighbors."

Jess laughed. "Yeah, but Negroes ain't real welcome in Little Italy."

Just then, there was a disturbance at the door. A huge, red-faced fellow came barreling through. He seized a man at one of the tables by the throat. They scuffled. Another man jumped in.

"Watch out, he's got a knife!" someone shouted.

The knife appeared, the blade gleaming in the poor light. Jess rushed forward and grabbed the waving arm. He held on tight as he tried to force it down. But the man broke free and pushed Jess away. Then he reached out, stabbed Jess in the chest, and ran.

Jess lay on the floor, motionless. Tony started toward him as the police arrived.

"All right, all right!" yelled the officer, "Who did this? Do we know? Do we care?"

There was silence for a moment. But in that moment, Tony knew what was coming from the Irish bartender. "It was the kid, the wop kid—that one, right there!"

"Yeah, the wop kid!" said someone in the crowd.

"Sorry, Jess," Tony whispered. Then he ran for the door.

160

"Hey, stop him!" he heard as he made it through the crowd. He ran up the Bowery in the dark. He kept running and running, knowing there was only one place he could run—one place he would be taken in if only he could get there in time.

He was almost there, but he was running out of breath. Nick Dale's Gramercy Park townhouse loomed up as if it were Heaven, the park a civilized oasis as Tony raced for the steps. He'd bobbed and weaved down several streets and lost the police completely. But how much time did he have? Chest heaving, he pounded on the door, hoping and praying that—

The door opened. Tony fell into Nick's arms.

Chapter 18

Was it hours later, or was it only minutes? Tony didn't know. All that mattered was that he was here, safe in this comfortable house, with someone who believed him. He sat now in Nick's living room, admiring the green velvet furniture, the paintings on the walls, and the polished wood tables. The soft glow of the lamplight gave an added dimension to the tranquil atmosphere.

Tony had never been in a room like this before, but he felt immediately at home. Nick had calmed him down, given him a glass of water, and listened to his story. Now he was sitting in an armchair asking, "Is there anyone who saw you, anyone who would take your side?"

Tony shook his head.

"Anyone besides me who could vouch for your character?"

"Jacob Riis."

"You know Jacob Riis?"

"Yes. At least I used to."

When Tony had finished his story about Riis, Nick said, "Why didn't you call him before? Why didn't you tell him what had happened to you?"

Tony could think of many reasons, but there was really only one. "I was too proud."

Nick shook his head. "Well, I'm going to call him now. Do you have the number?"

Tony dug into his pants pocket. It was still there, on a crumpled scrap of paper. "He lives in Richmond Hill."

The phone was in the study. Tony heard Nick dialing, then his urgent voice on the line. A moment later, Nick burst back into the living room.

"He was coming in tonight anyway. He'll meet us at the Mulberry Street police headquarters in an hour. He'd wondered why you'd disappeared."

"Me too," Tony said sadly. He surveyed his life, once again in tatters. He wondered if he'd end up in jail for something he didn't do.

But Nick was good at comfort, and by the time they left the house a half-hour later, Tony felt more confident.

They rode downtown in Nick's carriage, with two shiny black horses up front. Tony had never been in a carriage before. As they made their way through the starless New York night, he tried to imagine himself a visiting dignitary rather than a soon-to-be-arrested criminal. He was doing fine until they arrived at the corner of Mulberry and Houston. There was Jacob Riis in front of the building, wearing his familiar wing-collared shirt and elegant suit.

"Tony!" Riis said.

Tony almost broke down. He introduced Mr. Riis to Nick and described what had happened over the last few months.

Riis said, "You must never doubt me again, Tony. Now let's go inside and try to clear this up."

The three marched into police headquarters, but it was Jacob Riis who marched up to the desk. "Good evening, Officer Clancy," he said, shaking hands with the policeman on duty.

"Yes, sir, Mr. Riis," said the officer.

"I'm here with a young friend who says he has been wrongly accused of a crime. Is Lieutenant Donovan in? I'd like to speak to him about it."

Riis waved to Nick and Tony, then vanished into the rear of police headquarters. Nick and Tony retreated to a bench in the hallway to wait . . . and wait . . . and worry.

Riis couldn't have been gone more than 15 minutes. When he returned, he was smiling. "They caught the Irishman who did it. He was dead-drunk and confessed on the street. The Negro fellow is in the hospital. He's going to be all right. Tony, the charges against you have been dropped. You can go home."

Home, what home? Tony thought. But he felt as if he'd been rescued from the edge of a cliff. He shook Riis's hand. "Thank you, sir, thank you so much."

"It's all right, Tony. You just happened to be in the wrong place at the wrong time."

Nick was jubilant. "Why don't we all go back to my house to celebrate? Tony, I'm inviting you to spend the night."

Riis had to go across the street to check his schedule, but when he had, he said he could come. They all crowded into Nick's carriage. The horses' hooves pummeled the cobblestones, the large wheels rumbled. For a moment, Tony felt like a king returned to his throne.

Soon they were relaxing in Nick's comfortable living room—Jacob Riis almost disappearing into a velvet armchair and Nick carrying on about Tony's good fortune in knowing Mr. Riis. Nick's wife Erica, a blue-eyed woman with long auburn hair, joined them. So did their daughter Clarissa, who looked just like her mother but with wide green eyes. A maid offered them coffee and little cakes.

Soon Riis and Nick were involved in a long conversation about how to help the poor and Riis's admiration for the work of the Society. He handed Nick a cigar and took one himself, but as they continued talking Tony became uneasy. They were, after all, talking about the misfortunes of poor people. That meant, at least indirectly, that they were talking about Tony. He looked over at Clarissa, who smiled.

"Are you still in school?" he asked.

Clarissa told Tony she was 14 and attended a private

school in the city. She loved Gramercy Park. It was so enchanting.

Suddenly Riis was saying, "Tony, I didn't know you were so interested in education. You never mentioned it."

Nick had told Riis what Tony had never been able to say. So they really had been talking about him—in a good way!

"Yes, sir," Tony said.

"And what would you like to study?"

Caught off guard, Tony hesitated. Did he have an answer? Did he know? Everything in his head came together at once.

"I'd like to be a photographer."

Riis didn't miss a beat. "I know some people over at the LaSalle Institute on Second Avenue. I'm sure you could go either part-time or full-time, whatever works for you. Let me look into it."

Before Tony could reply, Nick said, "You're forgetting Tony's father."

"Oh, yes, Italian immigrant fathers!" Riis exclaimed. "I think it's time we helped Tony with his family situation."

They came up with a plan. By the time Tony went to bed—between real sheets, in a real bedroom—he couldn't believe that this night had really happened.

In the morning, he got up early to go to work. He wanted to say thank you, but everyone seemed asleep. As he was about to let himself out the door—turning the knob as quietly as possible—Clarissa appeared.

"Would you like some breakfast?" she asked.

Tony was flattered—and hungry. "I'd love some," he replied.

She seated him at the dining-room table and went into the kitchen. Moments later, the cook brought out eggs, bacon, toast, and coffee. Clarissa joined Tony at the table and they ate quietly, exchanging smiles between bites. As Tony got up to leave, their eyes locked.

"Delicious breakfast. Thank you," Tony blurted. Then he lunged toward the door and down the steps. It was a wonder he made it, a wonder he arrived at the *Tribune* to meet Sal. All the way there, those green eyes, that fabulous breakfast, and the impossibility of it all filled his imagination.

He told Sal nothing of what had happened last night. By tomorrow Sal would know everything about the plan, but today it was business as usual.

After work, Tony met Nick at the Duane Street Lodging House. Together they walked to Mulberry Street, climbed the terrible stairs, and knocked on the door of Apartment 5C.

Mamma answered. "Tonio!" she shouted and threw her arms around his neck.

Angelina was working at the kitchen table. "Tony, it's Tony!" she yelled.

Joey was there too. He jumped up, ran over, and threw his arms around Tony's waist. With two people hanging on to him, Tony half-walked, half-hopped to the table. They all sat down, and after more crying and embracing, Tony introduced Nick to everyone. Nick explained that he was from the Children's Aid Society and that Tony had been staying at the Duane Street Lodging House. "Tony misses his family terribly, Signora Petrosino," he added.

"You don't have to tell me," Mamma said, looking at her eldest son and patting his hand. "I just want him home."

Good. She would help.

Vinnie came in. Looking shocked, he hugged Tony tightly. "Are you going to stay?" he asked.

"I hope so," Tony replied.

It got dark. Waiting for Papà made Tony feel like he was gradually, hopelessly, sinking into a hole. A half-hour later, there was the sound of heavy boots on the stairs.

The door flew open. Papà surveyed the scene. "What are you doing here?" he said.

Will that be it? thought Tony.

Nick stepped in. He guided Papà to the sofa, sat Tony beside his father, and pulled up a chair for himself.

"Signor Petrosino, your son loves you very much," Nick began. "Every day without his family has been like a nightmare."

Papà blinked but was obviously listening. He seemed impressed that a man like Nick had come to speak for his son.

Nick went on, talking about the lodging house, about Tony's desire to be a photographer, and about Jacob Riis and the LaSalle Institute. All along—very carefully and politely—Tony translated the more complicated parts into Italian. The hardest moment came when Nick declared that Tony had not wished to insult his father and would not insult him again.

Would that be so? He'd already done it twice. Tony wanted to say something to confirm this but could not.

Soberly, Papà studied Tony's face.

"I want to be your son again," Tony said.

There was silence. Then after what seemed like forever, Papà said, "Yes, Tony, you may come home."

Tony cried out in happiness. He embraced his papà. He embraced Nick and Mamma and his brothers and sister. He convinced Nick to stay for dinner. And that night, after hours of hugging and catching up, he slept on the sofa and didn't mind at all.

Epilogue

A week later, Tony went back to the marionette theater on Spring Street as a performance was ending. He threaded his way through the crowd.

Maria was standing on the stage, talking with one of the puppeteers. He watched her for a moment, admiring her still and loving her. She turned, saw him, then turned her back.

So that was how it had to end. No explanation would be good enough, and there was no way he could see her again. Perhaps, as more time in America went by, as his future improved and he grew older, the rules might change. He hoped that would be so. He wanted it very much.

Author's Note

Jacob Riis went on to accomplish much of what he intended. In November 1890, his book, *How the Other Half Lives*, exposed conditions in the New York City tenements to a wide audience and helped generate, through text and photographs, tenement house reform. In 1894, the Gilder Tenement House Commission decreed that Mulberry Bend should be torn down. By 1897, a park had taken its place. In 1895, Riis convinced his friend Theodore Roosevelt, then police commissioner of New York City, to abolish the police station lodging houses. In later years, through books, journalism, and lectures all over America, Riis played an important part in the creation of better housing for the poor, child labor laws, and small parks and school playgrounds.

Castle Garden in the late 1800's